LAST CHRISTMAS

LAST CHRISTMAS

THE PRIVATE PREQUEL

KATE BRIAN

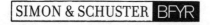

SIMON & SCHUSTER BFYR

New York   London   Toronto   Sydney

SIMON & SCHUSTER BFYR

An imprint of Simon & Schuster Children's Publishing Division
1230 Avenue of the Americas, New York, NY 10020

SIMON & SCHUSTER BOOKS FOR YOUNG READERS is a trademark
of Simon & Schuster, Inc.

alloyentertainment

Produced by Alloy Entertainment
151 West 26th Street
New York, NY 10001

Book design by Andrea C. Uva

Manufactured in the United States of America

2 4 6 8 10 9 7 5 3 1

CIP data for this book is available from the Library of Congress.

ISBN-13: 978-1-4169-1369-6
ISBN-10: 1-4169-1369-6

FIRST
EDITION

For Lanie, who brought it all together

LAST CHRISTMAS

White headlights severed the darkness as Ariana Osgood veered from the two-lane highway onto an overgrown road near the outskirts of Easton, Connecticut. She gripped the steering wheel with one hand and adjusted the rearview mirror with the other, glancing nervously into it.

Calm down, Ariana. Just calm down.

She hadn't been followed; she knew that. No one had seen her slip away from Billings House in Josh Hollis's Range Rover. No one knew that she was retracing the route she'd taken just an hour ago with Noelle Lange, Kiran Hayes, and Taylor Bell. That she was coming back for Thomas. And no one knew why she needed to find him. Her secrets—their secrets—were safe.

Rocks and chunks of hardened earth popped underneath the Range Rover's tires as she jerked the car off the road, cutting through the grassy field. She leaned forward and squinted into the blackness.

He was somewhere out there. She just had to find him, talk to him. And once she did, he would understand everything. Understand that he was wasting his time with Reed Brennan, that she was nothing but a novelty. A terrible mistake. Understand that he was meant to be with Ariana.

Suddenly her headlights caught something. Someone. Someone slumping limply from a pole.

Thomas.

"No!" She slammed on the brake pedal and swerved violently, barely missing him. Hands shaking, Ariana fumbled with the lock and opened the door, leaving the car's headlights on.

"Thomas!" Her voice sounded small in the open, deserted expanse around them. Thomas's head lolled forward, his chin grazing his chest. He groaned and mumbled something Ariana couldn't understand. Panic bubbled in her throat as she stared in disbelief at the figure in front of her, as if she was seeing him like this for the first time. Had they really left him in this condition? His arms and legs were tied to the pole with thick rope, and a black mesh bag was draped over his head. His chest and torso were covered with scratches from where her friends had jabbed him with tree branches. Dried blood encrusted a cut on his shoulder. The shirt he'd been wearing was on the ground, next to the baseball bat Noelle had forgotten to take with her when they'd left not even an hour ago.

Ariana's heart twisted painfully in her chest. How could she have let this happen? She'd never meant to hurt him, had only gone along with Noelle's plan so she wouldn't suspect anything.

"Thomas." The second her fingers grazed his clammy skin, he flinched, recoiling from the contact. From her. "Thomas, it's me," she choked, ripping the bag off his head. She had to cover her mouth to keep from vomiting. Thomas looked almost . . . dead. His wet curls were matted against his gray, sweaty face.

"I'm here. It's all right," she whispered, as much to herself as to him, and started to work on the knot binding his wrists. It didn't budge. "You're safe. I'm here to take care of you," she grunted, pulling futilely at the knot. She could have killed herself for not thinking to bring a knife or scissors.

His eyelids fluttered. "Take care of me?" he croaked.

"Of course." He would be so grateful to her for saving his life—for keeping their secret through all that—that he would never leave her again. Everything would go back to normal, and they could be together. Just like they'd planned. Just like he'd promised.

"Go to hell," he moaned.

The venom in his voice stung like a slap across the face. Thomas had never spoken to her like that. Digging her nails into her palms, she reminded herself that he was probably still drunk, or high. He didn't know what he was saying. He loved her, wanted to be with her. She knew he did. She just had to make him remember.

"Thomas, I just want to help." She sounded weak. She hated sounding weak. She reached for the rope coiled around his wrists and tugged at the knots. "I—"

"Don't touch me," he said, his voice stronger this time. His blue eyes bore into hers, full of disgust. "You think I don't know it was you who tied me up like this? You think I didn't recognize your voice?"

"It wasn't me! It was Noelle! I couldn't stop her!" His image blurred in front of her as tears filled her eyes. This couldn't be happening. After everything they'd been through together, it couldn't end like this. "I would never hurt you. I love you," she said, her voice a barely audible whisper. "You love me too. You have to." A salty tear slipped down her cheek.

"Or what?" he spat. His stare sliced through her like a steel blade. "What are you gonna do, Ariana? Kill me?" A strange laugh slipped from his lips. "Like you killed—"

"Stop it. You're drunk. You don't know what you're saying. You're not thinking clearly."

He shook his head, his desperate laugh still hanging in the air between them. "The thing is," he croaked, "for once in my life, I actually am. Everything is clear now that I have Reed in my—"

"Don't you dare say that name," Ariana snapped, digging her nails into her arms. Hot rage rose inside her. "She's not like us, and you know it. She's a nobody, Thomas. A nothing."

"She's everything!" Thomas yelled. He lunged forward, his chest heaving. "Don't you get it? She's everything you're not, Ariana. I love her."

"No, you love me!" Ariana screamed. "Everything I did, I did for you. For us."

"There *is* no *us*," Thomas spat.

"No us?" she repeated dumbly, taking a step back and wincing at her vulnerability. She fought to keep her voice steady. "Do you not love me?"

"Not anymore. Not after the things you did. The things *we* did." He was silent for a while. When he spoke again, his voice was calm. "But I'm going to fix it," he said quietly. "Make it right. I have to."

"What are you saying?" Her throat felt tight, like she couldn't get enough air. How could he not love her anymore? He had to. *Had* to. He was the reason she'd done those things. The reason why those things were okay. Worth it. How was she supposed to live without him? How was she supposed to continue to watch him with Reed? Her stomach heaved at the thought and she gasped for air.

In . . . two . . . three . . .

Out . . . two . . . three . . .

"I'm going to the police. I'm going to tell them everything. I'm coming clean—about you, about me. And maybe while I'm there I'll tell them what you and your little Billings friends did to me tonight, too."

"No. No, no, no." Ariana doubled over. This couldn't be happening. Couldn't. What had gone wrong? Why was he doing this? How could he not want her anymore? Not want to *protect* her? "You'll ruin everything. My life will be over. Please," she begged, stumbling toward him. She tripped over a rock and fell at his feet, heaving sobs emanating from her shaking body. "Please don't do this to me."

"I have to," he repeated slowly. The cut from his shoulder had started bleeding again. "For Reed. She deserves the truth."

"Thomas," Ariana moaned, collapsing into the cracked earth. Tears streamed down her dirty face. Everything she had worked so hard for was slipping away. Soon, she would be left with nothing. No one.

The blurred image of a baseball bat wavered in front of her, just inches away. She watched as her fingers closed around its wooden neck. Watched as she drew the bat closer and brought herself slowly to her feet. It was as if she was watching someone else. "I can't let you do this to me. I can't let you ruin me, *leave* me," she said quietly. It was someone else's voice. It wasn't hers. It couldn't be. She was Ariana Osgood. Easton Academy's Good Girl. "I'm sorry, but I just can't."

Fear and resignation seeped slowly into Thomas's face, his voice. "You're fucking insane," he said quietly. "I should have known."

"Shut up, Thomas." She raised the bat over her head.

"Just like your mother." He looked her directly in the eye and spat at her.

"Stop it!" she shrieked. The tears were coming harder now. "I'm nothing like her! Nothing!"

"You were never good enough for me. For anyone."

You never know what people are capable of until they're pushed to their edge, Ariana.

"You're crazy. You're insa—"

The sickening crack of the bat against Thomas's ribs startled her. A primitive, guttural scream escaped from her soul as she felt his body give way under her hands. His cries intertwined with her own, until she couldn't tell them apart. The begging, the pleading, the hollow thud of the bat swelled around her. She needed silence. A single moment of peace. She raised the bat over her head once more and closed her eyes.

And everything went black.

THE GOOD GIRL
DECEMBER OF JUNIOR YEAR

Ariana Osgood just wanted to go home.

She knew it was insane. She was, after all, standing at the edge of the ballroom at the Driscoll Hotel, playing witness to the most decadent party of the year. The party she had circled in red on her social calendar three months ago and had been looking forward to every day since. But now that she was at the Winter Ball, watching all of Easton Academy mingle and chat and dance, all she wanted to do was go back to Billings House and be with her friends. Her sisters. Inside Billings it was simple. Inside Billings she could just be.

Ariana reached up and touched her light blond hair, making sure for the fiftieth time that the chignon she'd worked so hard to achieve had held. How could she have forgotten how these events always put her on edge? Always made her feel hot and clenched and breathless. She was going to say something stupid. Or do something wrong. And everyone would see. Everyone would know.

Which was why she had spent the past fifteen minutes leaning against a grooved marble column on the outskirts of the room, just out of view of the table where her friends and boyfriend, Daniel Ryan, were sitting. Sooner or later they were going to notice her marathon bathroom trips and the current column-hugging, and she was going to have to rejoin their reveling. Better make these last few minutes of invisibility count.

Taking a deep breath, Ariana let the sounds of laughter and clinking silverware fade into the recesses of her mind and watched the scene around her unfold like a movie on mute. She committed every detail of the black and white marble room to memory as if her life depended on it. Noting details, cataloging a scene, always made her feel calm, in control.

There were her classmates, stiff and formal in their suits and dresses. The twelve-piece band singing pop versions of Christmas carols on the stage up front. The light December snow falling outside, the large flakes kissing the leaded windowpanes. The waxy mistletoe and the candlelit wreaths that—if she squinted her eyes just so— looked like explosions of gold.

But the curtains . . . well, those she had to remember down to the last filigreed stitch so she could report back to her mother about them. They were exquisite, all burgundy velvet with shimmering gold-thread fleurs-de-lis. Her mother, a New Orleans native, loved fleurs-de-lis. When Ariana was nine, her mother had given her a gorgeous gold fleur-de-lis necklace for Christmas. That had been Ariana's favorite Christmas. The last happy one she could remember.

The last one before her father started taking those extended business trips. Before her mother started to fade away. Ariana had never taken the antique necklace off, as if it could somehow tie her to those happier times.

"Whoops, sorry!" A drunk junior in a rumpled Betsey Johnson dress knocked into Ariana on the way to the bathroom, giggling and slurring and groping with her acne-scarred date.

With a blink, Ariana returned to her body, and the sounds of the ballroom rushed her ears at full volume. The band was playing "All I Want for Christmas," and a girl let out a shrill shriek as her boyfriend lifted her off her feet and spun her around. Ariana sighed and pushed away from the cool comfort of the column, giving her teeth a quick flick with her tongue to clear away any wayward lip gloss as she wove her way through the crowd.

As she slowly approached her table, Ariana took a mental picture of her friends. The Billings Girls. She loved to watch them from afar, study their mannerisms, note their tics and gestures and habits. More than anything, she loved when she caught them doing something gross or stupid when they thought no one was watching. Like picking their teeth, or adjusting their boobs in their dresses, or checking out cute-but-dorky Drake boys from across the room. She liked to make mental lists of their imperfections. It made her feel less imperfect herself.

Of course, finding imperfections among the Billings Girls was never easy. It took a practiced eye. They were, after all, Easton royalty. Which meant that Ariana was Easton royalty. She had been ever since September, when she'd taken her place as a junior member of Easton's most elite dorm. Now the Billings Girls, the ones her mother had always talked about as if they were characters in a fairy tale, were her dorm mates. Her friends. Her sisters.

When Ariana was just a few feet away, she noticed that Isobel Bautista, a senior who had taken Ariana under her wing at the beginning of the year, was playing with her violet D&G heels under the table, letting them swing from her toes as she gazed around the ballroom. Suddenly the right one fell off and landed a few inches away from her foot. Ariana watched as Isobel scooched down in her chair as casually as possible to retrieve it. As she was fishing around with her toes, she brushed Noelle Lange's ankle, and Noelle whacked her boyfriend Dash McCafferty's arm.

"You're playing footsie with me? What are we, twelve?" Noelle joked.

"Wasn't me," Dash replied, flashing a killer smile. "But I'll play anytime you want."

Isobel finally shoved her foot into her shoe and sat up again, admitting to nothing, but the snapshot of normality soothed Ariana. She smiled and finally joined them.

"There you are," Noelle said, flipping her thick, dark mane of hair over her shoulder as Ariana slipped into her chair. Noelle was, as always, wearing her signature black—a sleek satin Adam & Eve dress that showed off all her curves. "I was beginning to think you'd nicked a bottle of Dash's contraband Cristal and gone streaking through the streets of Easton."

Noelle took a sip of champagne from her crystal flute—the

champagne Dash had paid off the waiters to serve their table in lieu of sparkling cider, since alcohol was prohibited at school functions—and then took a bite of a chocolate-covered strawberry. Noelle was Ariana's best friend at Easton. They balanced each other well. Noelle was more brazen and confident, where Ariana was more reserved and cautious. During their hazing period at Billings, Noelle had helped Ariana through more than one crisis of confidence, while Ariana had helped Noelle refrain from telling off the older sisters on more than one occasion. She was sure that neither of them would have made it through initiation without the other.

"Noelle, streaking is so gauche," Ariana admonished as she took a seat beside Daniel. She smoothed her white, layered Alberta Ferretti dress over her knees and wrapped her hands around the seat of her raw silk–covered chair. "I was just taking it all in. The social committee did an incredible job."

"I swear, if you start rhapsodizing about the engraving on the silverware, I *will* kill you." Noelle groaned and slipped a silver mono-grammed flask from her beaded Marc Jacobs clutch.

"I think it's cute when you go all poetic," Daniel said, draping his arm across the back of Ariana's chair. Ariana looked up at his chiseled profile, his auburn hair, his ridiculously long lashes, and felt for the millionth time the triumph of having a boyfriend like him. They'd been a couple for more than a year, and she still marveled that he had chosen her over all the other girls at Easton. "And Noelle . . ." He tipped his champagne flute toward her. "If you kill my girlfriend, you can kiss Dash good-bye."

"It's Christmas. There will be no killing on my watch," Ariana said.

"Buzzkill." Noelle offered the flask to Dash, but he waved it off.

"I have an early day tomorrow," he said, checking his thick silver watch. He ran his hands through his wavy blond hair and blew out a sigh. "I have to be in Boston at six a.m. to meet my father."

"Six a.m.? You are a saint, Dash McCafferty," Paige Ryan said as Noelle handed her the flask instead.

Dash blushed, even with Noelle watching. Paige just had that kind of power over people. Her great-great-grandmother Jessica Billings had founded Billings House more than eighty years ago. Paige, with her auburn curls and glass green eyes, *was* Billings. The true leader. The girl who made even Noelle pause with uncertainty. She was also Daniel's twin sister.

"So what did I miss?" Ariana asked.

"About ten minutes of your boyfriend talking about your Christmas vacation plans. It was lethally boring—even worse than when you get into your Emily Dickinson moods." Noelle rolled her dark eyes. A black-vested waiter silently reached over her shoulder, clearing plates and neatly laying dessert forks over fresh napkins.

Daniel gave Ariana a quick kiss. "Vermont is going to rock," he said with a wink.

Ariana gave Daniel a tight smile, her heart suddenly leaden in her chest. She knew what that wink meant. She and Daniel had long ago decided that they would lose their virginity to each other on their one-year anniversary. But when said anniversary had rolled around back in November, Ariana had chickened out. Of course, she hadn't let Daniel know she was scared. She had simply insisted that she was not about to lose her virginity in a dorm room. Daniel had been disappointed but understanding. The very next day he had invited her to spend the holidays with him and his family at some gorgeous ski lodge in Vermont, promising some serious *alone time.*

Ariana knew what that meant. It meant no more excuses.

The question was, why wasn't she excited about it? After all, Daniel was perfect. He won Firsts every semester, was captain of the lacrosse team and model-cute, and had already been accepted to Harvard early decision. But the thought of having sex with him made her feel as if she'd swallowed a herd of elephants. That couldn't be normal. Any girl would kill to be in her position, to have a boyfriend like Daniel. What was wrong with her? She studied her napkin—white, silk, Italian—until the feeling passed.

"Well, I'm jealous." Isobel adjusted the strap of her deep purple satin dress. "My parents are ditching me for Turks and Caicos. I'm campus-bound until Christmas."

"You can come to New York with me if you want," Noelle offered with a shrug. "My parents won't even notice you're there."

I wish I could take her up on that, Ariana thought, then immediately felt guilty. She picked one of the decorative red and gold–wrapped boxes off the table and ran the ribbons between her fingernails until they curled.

"Or you could come to Vermont with us," Paige said with a toss of her hair.

She was just passing the flask to Ariana when Thomas Pearson appeared out of nowhere and grabbed it from her fingers. He dropped into the empty chair between Ariana and Paige and took a swig.

"Good stuff," he said, clearing his long brown bangs away from his eyes with a casual flick of his head. "But then, you girls always have the good stuff, don't you?"

"Great. Now I'm going to have to have it sterilized," Noelle groused, leaning over the table to snatch the flask.

Thomas turned and smiled at Ariana, his deep blue eyes merry. She silently cursed her bad luck. Thomas had always made her uncomfortable. The way he thought he was better than everyone else. The way he constantly teased her. The fact that he was a loser drug dealer with no respect for anyone around him . . .

"Sterilized, get it?" he said to Ariana, his tone deadpan. He loosened his black tuxedo tie and slung one arm over the back of his chair. "Because I'm ridden with germs. She's hilarious."

Ariana shifted her gaze and inched away from Thomas and closer to Daniel, tucking her shoulder into the crook of his arm.

"Seriously, come to Vermont," Paige said to Isobel, ignoring Thomas as she always did. Even though he was Dash's best friend and came from one of New York's best families, Paige never gave him the time of day. "Save me from being the third wheel to the sappy couple over here," she added, gesturing at Ariana and Daniel with a strawberry.

"Aw, you're just bitter because Brady dumped you the second he got to Yale," Daniel teased his sister.

Paige's eyes flashed angrily. "Excuse me, I did not get dumped. *I broke up with* him."

Everyone glanced around the table. They all knew that Brady Flynn had booted Paige. Several Yale-bound Easton alums had witnessed the dumping and instantly texted their friends about it. But of course no one would contradict Paige—to her face, anyway.

"So what's the Lange family's Christmas protocol?" Isobel asked Noelle, deftly changing topics before Paige exploded. The last time Paige lost her temper, it had not been pretty. During chores one morning post-breakup she had reduced the normally tough Leanne Shore to tears, demanding she remake Paige's bed ten times until the hospital corners were at perfect ninety-degree angles. Afterward Leanne had spent an hour in the nurse's office with her inhaler, fighting off a panic attack.

Ariana was proud that she had never broken down like that during hazing. Not in public, anyway.

"The ballet, cocktails with my father's miserable excuse for an attorney and his overstuffed wife. The usual," Noelle said. "My parents will probably try to sneak in a little face time with the extracurriculars and write it off as Christmas shopping, meaning they have to buy me more presents. They get a little ass, I get a little Armani. It's a win-win."

Noelle talked about her parents' affairs like she was giving an oral report on the Industrial Revolution. As if there were nothing in the world that could have been more mundane. Ariana fingered one of her aquamarine drop earrings, envying how everything was so easy, so straightforward for her best friend.

"I can't imagine what that's like, worrying about when your parents are going to schedule in their 'face time' with their sloppy sides." Daniel leaned back as the waiter delivered coffee cups and bowls of sugar to the table. "That's gotta suck."

Ariana inhaled sharply. No one at this table needed a reminder about how happy and functional the Ryan family unit was. Noelle's dark eyes smoldered at the dig.

"Well, Daniel, not everyone can have the perfect family, perfect grades, and the perfect girlfriend," Thomas said wryly, teasing Ariana with his eyes.

"If we did, what would we tell our therapists about?" Dash joked.

"Or pop Xanax over," Thomas added with a short laugh.

"Like you need an excuse to pop anything," Noelle put in.

Thomas smiled. "Touché, Miss Lange." He snagged a sugar cube from the bowl and tossed it into his mouth. "What about you, Ariana. Popped anything lately?"

Prickly heat assaulted Ariana's skin.

"Dude," Daniel admonished, sitting forward to glare at Thomas.

"What?" Thomas feigned innocence with upturned palms.

Ariana forced herself to glance at Thomas. He was looking directly at her with his searing blue eyes.

Just then a camera flashed, illuminating the beveled edges of her glass with sparks of light. Ariana flinched.

"Jesus," Noelle snapped, waving her napkin in the direction of the flash. "Sergei, enough with the stalkerazzi act already. Find new muses."

Sergei Tretyakov stood just two feet from the table, a black Nikon with a telephoto lens hanging from his neck. Sergei was a Latvian exchange student and an outsider at Easton. He had dark, sloping brows, coal black eyes, and a slightly crooked nose. He could have been quirkily attractive, but he was painfully shy and had a tendency to stare. Plus he always wore these old, dirty tennis shoes no matter what else he had on. He was even wearing them tonight, to a formal event. Ariana could tell a lot about a person from their choice of footwear, and Sergei's kicks screamed "street urchin." Still, she felt a certain reluctant affinity for him. She was, after all, a fellow observer.

"Just one more," he said softly in his lilting Eastern European accent.

This time, he pointed the camera directly at Ariana and snapped away. Ariana blushed at being singled out.

Daniel stood up, his chair scraping loudly against the marble floor. "Dude, did you just take a picture of my girlfriend?"

The table went silent and Ariana could feel Noelle's eyes on her. She stopped breathing.

Not again . . . not again . . . not again . . .

Ariana watched Sergei's face go ashen. He backed away slightly, his shoulders curled forward.

"I've taken everyone's picture tonight." Sergei was like a cowering puppy in the face of an irate owner. Ariana couldn't take it. Besides, the last thing she wanted was a scene like the one that had played out in the woods last summer. Not here. Not now.

"Daniel, it's fine. Don't worry about it," she said in a soothing voice.

But Daniel wasn't having it. "No, it's not fine." He fixed his eyes on Sergei and crossed his arms over his chest. "Do you think my girl-friend's pretty?"

Sergei blinked uncertainly. "Well . . . I . . . yes?" It came off like a question.

Daniel's cheek twitched. Several waiters brought out tartlets and crème brûlée on silver trays, filling the room with the scent of smoked apples and nutmeg.

"So what do you like best about my girlfriend? Her smile? Her hair?" Daniel's eyes gleamed. "Her cleavage?"

Thomas and Dash hid smirks behind their hands. Noelle and Paige stood up, rolling their eyes at the display of testosterone, and headed toward the bathroom. Isobel whipped out her Sidekick and started texting, probably alerting the other students in the room to the main event unfolding at table one.

"Daniel, stop," Ariana said quietly as Sergei stared at the floor.

"And do you take pictures of all the pretty girls?" Daniel asked, a condescending smile playing on his full lips. "Or is it just my girl-friend?"

"I think I'll go now," Sergei said, backing away from the table.

Ariana flinched as Daniel grabbed Sergei's arm. "Just a second, buddy."

With one quick motion, he lifted Sergei's camera over his head and started scrolling through the stored images. Sergei made a swipe for the camera, but Daniel held it out of reach.

"Oh, here's a picture of Ariana, and another and another. Isobel—

you're in here too. And that's a nice one of Natasha. Hmm. No guys in any of these. Interesting. You know, you're lucky I don't call the cops on you, pervert."

Thomas snickered quietly.

"That's enough," Ariana said firmly, her cheeks flushed and heart racing.

Daniel stared at her for a second, his eyes hard, angry, empty. Then his whole body went slack and he punched Sergei in the shoulder. "Kidding, man. I'm just giving you a hard time."

"So can I have my camera back then?" Sergei looked bewildered.

"A little later," Daniel said with a wink. "I think it's best if I keep it for now."

The band switched to a slow song and the air suddenly smelled like hazelnut coffee. Sergei held out his hand. "You can't just take my camera."

Daniel sat back down and cocked his head to the side. "Dude, you can't just take pictures of my girlfriend."

Sergei looked torn for a second as he stared longingly at his Nikon, then turned away. In his haste to leave he nearly knocked over a waitress refilling water glasses at a nearby table. She glared at him and sopped up the spill with a napkin.

"You shouldn't have done that." Ariana took a sip of champagne, hoping Isobel's message hadn't reached too many people. Hoping they hadn't noticed that her boyfriend had just senselessly humiliated the awkward exchange student.

Daniel held his hands up and laughed. "Hey, I was just messing with the guy. Besides, he shouldn't being taking pictures of you. Not without asking, anyway. Guy has to learn a little respect." His voice turned serious, and he put his hand on her knee. It felt cold and heavy. Possessive. "You know I'd do anything for you, Ari. Anything. Don't forget that."

Ariana smiled tightly. "I won't."

Daniel's words should have sounded sweet and loving. But as Ariana caught a glimpse of Sergei across the room, looking naked and vulnerable without his camera, she couldn't help but hear them as a threat.

PERFECT

Ariana looked at her watch. Twelve twenty-seven a.m. She tried to fight the irritation that prickled along her skin. Her friends had left a half hour ago, her feet ached from her ivory Chloé heels, and the ballroom was nearly empty, save for a few stragglers and hotel maintenance workers, dutifully clearing tables and sweeping the floors.

Stifling a yawn, Ariana surveyed the damage around her. Half-empty crystal flutes rimmed with fading Chanel-lipstick pouts littered the tables. The tapered candles that peeked from the Christmasy centerpieces had melted into nothing, and the sharp smell of burnt vanilla and wilting greenery hovered in the air. The chandelier that had seemed magical earlier in the evening now cast a garish light over the tired waitstaff. The room suddenly looked ordinary. Used. Ariana felt an inexplicable pang of sadness as she sipped the last bit of flat champagne from her glass.

"Party's over, Osgood."

Ariana jumped at the sound of Thomas's voice. He sat down heavily next to her on the bench near the ballroom's exit, his arms crossed over his wrinkled dress shirt. His blue eyes were slightly unfocused, and it was clear he'd had too much to drink.

"So why are you still here?" She crossed her legs and placed her champagne flute on the floor. Thomas smelled like whiskey and something vaguely spicy.

"Well, I'm certainly not waiting for my boyfriend, who's currently puking his guts out in the bushes. Because that'd be lame." Thomas sniffed and rolled up one of his sleeve cuffs.

Ariana tugged on her necklace, moving it back and forth on its delicate chain. A tiny part of her agreed with Thomas. She should have taken up Noelle's offer to ride home with her and Dash. But then she thought about how Paige had glared at the suggestion—a not-so-subtle reminder that it was Ariana's duty as girlfriend to take care of Daniel. She just wished he hadn't challenged Gage Coolidge to that power hour. Because then she could be home right now, tucked between her sateen sheets.

She turned to Thomas. "What were *you* doing out in the bushes?"

"Oh, you know, a little of this, a little of that. Bushes are *always* fun." Thomas smirked suggestively. "You've heard of fun, right?"

"I do recall hearing of the concept," Ariana replied flatly, trying to step up to his banter.

"Right. I can definitely see you getting stupid and crazy," he said sarcastically.

Ariana's face grew warm. "I've done plenty of stupid and crazy things."

"True. You *are* dating Daniel Ryan," he replied.

"Ha ha," Ariana said, then realized with a pang how immature she sounded. Across the room a waiter dropped a wineglass. He swore, then bent down to pick up the jagged fragments. "Daniel and I are very happy," she added.

Thomas put his elbows on his knees and leaned forward. "So you thought his little tête-à-tête with Sergei was, what? Gallant?"

"He was drunk," Ariana pointed out. "And if I remember correctly, you were laughing." She unhooked her vintage Gucci bag from her shoulder and put it on her lap. Her container of Tic Tacs rattled inside. "I was laughing at Daniel, not at Sergei." Thomas ran his fingers through his hair. One side stuck out a little over his ear, making him look, ever so briefly, like a vulnerable little boy in his rumpled formalwear. "So, are you ready to 'rock' in Vermont?" he asked with a knowing grin.

Ariana felt like the words were a challenge. Even though her stomach twisted at the thought of losing her virginity to Daniel, she lifted her chin and said coolly, "I can't wait."

A worker in his mid-twenties grabbed an empty bottle of Perrier off one of the tables, dropping it with a clank into the recycling bag he was dragging behind him.

"Really? 'Cause you look like you're about to join Danny boy for a group vomit in the bushes."

"You're disgusting."

"Disgusting, but right." Thomas smirked. He pulled an old New York subway token out of his pocket and rolled it back and forth across the wood of the bench. It left a little black streak on the pristine oak finishing. "You do know you can do better."

Even though Ariana knew he wasn't serious, knew he was just teasing her as always, she couldn't help feel a flutter at the compliment.

"Daniel is the perfect boyfriend." Ariana met Thomas's blue eyes with her own.

"Maybe on paper," Thomas retorted.

And he was right. Ariana knew he was right. Daniel *was* perfect on paper, but sometimes, in reality, not so much. Like tonight. Getting drunk and treating Sergei like dirt and ignoring her when she asked him to stop. Not so perfect.

But she would never admit that to Thomas.

"Please. He just had a little too much to drink. On a normal day, he's amazing," Ariana told him, pressing her hands into the bench at her sides and looking straight ahead. "Like last night, he knew I had a ton of work to catch up on so he brought me dinner in my room—plus a couple dozen roses"

"Ooh. How original."

"It was—"

"Whatever. I don't want to talk about Daniel Ryan." Thomas leaned back, lacing his fingers behind his head. "I want to talk about you."

"Me." Ariana was nonplussed.

"Yeah. What's the worst thing you've ever done?"

"The worst thing?" Ariana leaned back too, molding her back

along the slats of the bench. She made a mental list of the things Paige
and her friends had forced the new girls to do to prove their devotion to Billings. Like the time Paige had made her break into Hell Hall
with a Sharpie and black out parts of the assistant headmaster's name
plaque so that it read ASS MASTER.

He started to whistle the theme to *Jeopardy*.

"Stop it," Ariana said.

"I want to hear something real. Something bad. Something hot." His
voice dropped to a whisper, and he nudged her knee with his. Ariana
froze. The light contact sent her skin humming. Suddenly his face was
only inches from her own. She could feel his breath on her neck. Her
own breath caught in her throat. "Come on, Osgood. Shock me."

"Well . . ." Ariana stalled, working to retain her composure and
calm her racing heart. It was hard, though, with Thomas's eyes prob-
ing every inch of her body, as if uncovering every last one of her many
secrets. She felt exposed. Naked. Exhilarated.

What would he do if she reached up and touched his cheek?

For a moment she felt dizzy, heady with the possibility that she
could actually do it. He was right there. They were alone, relatively.
He wouldn't be able to tease her anymore if she did something that
risky. Yeah, that would wipe that knowing smirk right off his incredibly handsome face.

Ariana felt her hands twitch with anticipation and shoved them
under her thighs.

What was wrong with her? This was *Thomas Pearson*. Everyone
knew he was a player. The kind of guy who hooked up with girls as long

as they amused him, then moved on once he decided he was bored. The kind of guy who hadn't batted an eye when his best friend, Eli Tate, had gotten expelled last year after the dean found him high in his room next to a half-empty bottle of Xanax—a bottle that everyone knew Thomas had sold him. More than that, she was supposed to be in love with *Daniel*.

But for some inexplicable reason, she couldn't turn away from Thomas. Couldn't break eye contact. Couldn't help but want to do something wrong for once. Couldn't help but want *him*.

"Someone's thinking naughty thoughts," Thomas sang in a whisper, gazing at Ariana's lips.

Ariana's entire body tingled. She opened her mouth to speak, not knowing what she was going to say.

"Ariana!" Daniel's bark obliterated the moment. "Let's get the hell out of here."

Ariana instantly slid all the way to the other end of the bench, as if Thomas had just burned her with a hot iron. Had Daniel seen anything? Not that there was anything to see, but—

"Wow. When he says 'jump,' do you say 'how high?'" Thomas teased.

Ariana narrowed her eyes at him, even as her heart pounded a painfully fast beat.

"Be there in a second," she called to Daniel. But he had already disappeared back into the hallway.

Suddenly all Ariana could feel was the sting of Daniel's disinterest. Wouldn't most guys be a little bit concerned if they spotted their

girlfriend alone on a bench with a guy like Thomas? It was embarrassing. And Thomas had noticed it too. There was nothing Thomas
Pearson didn't notice.

Suddenly, Ariana knew what she had to do. She turned to Thomas,
a smile tugging at her lips.

"Sorry to disappoint, but I guess I *am* a good girl. Always have
been, always will be." And with that, she placed her hand on his leg,
letting her fingertips graze the length of his thigh as she slowly stood
up. She couldn't believe she was doing this—especially with Daniel
right outside.

Apparently, neither could Thomas, whose eyes were wide with
shock. The air felt thick with electricity, and Ariana could feel her
pulse in her fingers. Her throat. Her heart. Everywhere. Touching
him, even if just for a second, felt inevitable. Like there was nothing
else she could do *but* touch him. Breathing heavily, Thomas reached
out, as if to take her hand, but Ariana stepped away. She turned her
back on him and walked to meet Daniel in the hallway, heady with
triumph. She had shocked Thomas Pearson. Mr. Aloof himself.

Apparently she was capable of such things.

"Sorry to make you wait. You okay, babe?" Daniel asked, putting
his hand on the small on her back and steering her toward the hotel's
exit.

"Fine," she lied. She actually felt faint and vaguely ill from the
gravity of what she had just done—the line she had just crossed.
She had done something unpredictable. Something off-script and
unplanned.

And she had enjoyed it.

But now, as they entered the empty lobby and Daniel took her hand in his, the spell was broken and guilt crashed over her in waves. Only a horrible person could think about a guy other than her boyfriend, even for a second—and at a Christmas dance, no less.

"Have I mentioned tonight that I love you?" Daniel asked, holding the front door open for her. A sleek black car sat in circular drive, the driver waiting patiently at the curb.

Ariana looked up at Daniel, searching his angular features and Brooks Brothers tux, looking for a stain, a scar, a flaw. There was none. Even post-booting he was perfect.

"I love you too," she murmured, giving him a quick kiss on the cheek. In that moment, she decided that whatever had happened with Thomas was nothing. Stupid. Meaningless. The result of too much champagne. Daniel was her boyfriend. Her life. The right guy.

She repeated the words over and over in her head, believing them each time. But when she stepped out into the freezing December night air, she realized that her leg still burned where Thomas had touched her.

MORE

"She needs something more," Ariana murmured aloud on Sunday afternoon. "Something he can't give her."

She swiveled in her desk chair, turning away from her laptop and the unfinished Word document that was taunting her. She snapped on the Christmas lights she and Noelle had strung around their dormered windows and watched as dusk began to settle over the campus. It was getting dark earlier and earlier each day. "So is it really wrong for her to look for romance somewhere else, if she knows she'll never truly be happy with him?"

"Depends." Noelle emerged from the walk-in closet they shared, peeking over the tower of designer threads she was carrying in her arms. "Maybe she isn't trying hard enough. Have they tried doing it in public?" She expertly navigated the mess of clothes that littered her half of the room, dumping the stash from the closet into an open Louis Vuitton suitcase on her unmade bed. "Because whenever I start to get a little bored with Dash, we go someplace where we know we might get caught. Ups the naughty factor. Or if she has a camcorder, she could—"

"Not *that* kind of romance," Ariana groaned, spinning back toward her desk. She tossed an old issue of *Quill*, the Easton literary magazine she contributed to, on the floor and typed one sentence into her computer. "And remind me never to borrow a movie from you without making sure it's not homemade."

"Noted." Noelle opened her top dresser drawer and pulled out several tubes of M.A.C. lip gloss.

Ariana picked up the pomegranate-cassis pillar candle Daniel had given her that morning as an early-Christmas-slash-sorry-I-got-drunk-last-night present and inhaled its waxy scent. "Anyhow, I'm talking about real romance. The kind of romance where you feel a burning desire to be with the person all the time."

"Who are we talking about, anyway?" Noelle asked, zipping up her red Vera Bradley makeup bag before grabbing a pair of caramel brown leather boots near the doorway.

"Emma Bovary," Ariana said. "And don't even think about taking my Michael Kors boots home with you. I need them for Vermont." She put the candle back down on her desk next to the three silver-framed photographs. They were her favorite pictures. One was a photo Paige had taken of her and Daniel last summer at the Ryans' Martha's Vineyard estate. The second was a black-and-white photo of Ariana by herself, taken by Daniel at Noelle's house in the Hamptons last summer, as Ariana blew a kiss at the camera. The other was an old candid of Ariana and her mother on the back porch of the family's sprawling home in Atlanta. They were both smiling, happy. It had been taken years ago, before her father had essentially checked out of their marriage. Before all the hospitalizations. Before Easton. Before Billings. It felt like another time, another life. The girl in the photo might as well have been another person. But Ariana loved the image just the same.

"Emma Bovary?" Noelle held a shimmering bronze minidress in front of her and pursed her lips at the full-length mirror on the closet door. "You mean that sophomore slut who slept with Gage after finals last year? Because he felt a burning sensation after he was with her, but I can guarantee you it wasn't desire."

"That was Emma Benning," Ariana corrected, forcing herself to look away from the photograph. "I'm talking about Emma Bovary as in *Madame Bovary.*" She waved her worn copy of the novel in the air. "As in, the tragic heroine of one of the most celebrated and controversial French novels of all time. We're reading it in Mr. Holmes's lit class, and we have a paper due before break."

Noelle yawned and glanced at the glowing alarm clock next to her silk-covered bed. "You just spent two minutes telling me a story about a depressed Frenchwoman who can't even get her husband to screw her?" She crossed her arms over her cream cashmere V-neck. "That's one hundred and twenty seconds of my life I'll never get back," she chided, throwing the dress into her suitcase. "So I'll be taking those Michael Kors boots with me as reimbursement."

Ariana didn't even bother to argue as Noelle shoved the boots into her bag. If she decided she really cared that much, she would simply sneak in there later tonight when Noelle was in deep-sleep mode and take them back. It was their way.

"It's actually an incredible book," Ariana sighed, lowering the book to her lap. "But this paper is incredibly bad." She drummed her fingers on the desk and deleted the last sentence she'd written. "It's only supposed to be a few pages, but I can't concentrate long enough to write a coherent sentence."

"Please. You know that Holmes will give you an A anyway. All you need to pass his class is a decent ass," Noelle said. She tilted her head, checking out Ariana's butt. "That's at least a B-plus."

"Thanks a lot." Ariana rolled her eyes.

"What's wrong? Worrying about the trip?" Noelle sat on her suitcase and tugged at the zipper. It didn't move.

"A little," Ariana admitted. Of course Noelle knew. Noelle *always* knew. It was almost like she had a sixth sense for gossip and other peoples' insecurities.

"Nervous about meeting the parents? I hear they're a little stuffy, but fine." She leaned over and brushed a piece of lint from her black patent leather Louboutins, her dark hair falling like a curtain over her face. "At least Daniel invited you. Dash's parents would never let me horn in on their holiday plans. God forbid a McCafferty holiday photograph ever differed one iota from the year before. I shudder to think what'll happen when grandkids come along. They'll probably have a kids' photo and an adults' photo. I mean, really. Would it be that big a deal to have *one* extra person hanging around?"

"Noelle Lange." Ariana twisted her hair into a bun and stuck a pencil through it. "Are you jealous?"

Noelle hesitated for a split second and Ariana knew that no matter what Noelle said next, she had hit the nail directly on the head. It was rare that Noelle showed a chink in the armor, and Ariana savored the moment.

"Don't be ridiculous," Noelle said. "I don't get jealous." She gave up on the zipper and sat down on the floor to sort through another pile of clothes. "And besides, we weren't talking about me. We were talking about you. And how you're so nervous to meet Daniel's parents that you can't even pull together a few pages of decent bullshit."

"It's not that," Ariana said slowly, using her mouse to highlight everything she'd written about Madame Bovary's more-than-questionable ethics. Her finger hovered uncertainly over the delete key. "I'm sure his parents are fine." She lowered her finger and pressed the button. Her failed efforts of the past few days disappeared, leaving a clean, blank screen. Ariana instantly felt better. It was nice when mistakes were so easily wiped away.

"So what is it, then?" Noelle asked impatiently. "You're acting like you don't even want to go. The place sounds amazing. It's supposed to be extremely—"

"Exclusive," Ariana finished for her, slamming her laptop screen closed in exasperation. "Believe me, I've heard. And it's not that I don't want to go. It's just that I'm a little nervous about . . ." She paused and glanced down at her lap. "About Daniel."

"Nervous about Daniel?" Noelle echoed. "Why? You're going to be with your hot boyfriend at an exquisite resort doing nothing but skiing, sitting around the lodge, and . . ." She paused, a devilish grin spreading across her face. "Having sex. And now I get it."

Ariana buried her face in her hands. "Ugh. What's wrong with me?"

"Just pre-virginity-loss jitters." Noelle shrugged and threw a Hermès scarf at Ariana. "Stop thinking about it and just *do* it already."

Ariana picked up the scarf and wrapped it around her neck. "But I just want to make sure it feels right."

"It's definitely not going to feel right," Noelle offered matter-of-factly. "It's going to feel like hell. So you have a few glasses of wine first, and it's over before you know it."

"That's not what I mean." Ariana flopped down on her bed and wrapped her arms around her squishiest pillow. "I just don't want to regret anything about my first time."

"You really have to deal with this obsessive need of yours to control every aspect of every situation," Noelle said, amused. "And besides, what's to regret? Daniel Ryan is the *perfect* guy. And he loves you. Everybody knows it."

"I know," Ariana sighed. She wound a lock of her wavy hair around her index finger and pulled it tight. She wanted to tell Noelle that she wasn't certain she loved Daniel back, but she kept her gaze fixed on the ceiling. She couldn't bring herself to say the words. She knew how Noelle would look back at her. Like Ariana had lost her mind. Like she was crazy.

"Ariana," Noelle said quietly, sitting down at the foot of Ariana's bed. "Almost every girl at this school would kill to be you."

Implication: every girl at this school with the exception of Noelle, who was perfectly happy being herself.

"Daniel is totally and completely right for you," Noelle continued. "So stop freaking out."

"You're right," Ariana sighed.

"Aren't I always?" Noelle held out her hand, and Ariana gave her back the Hermès scarf. "I'm meeting Dash. When I get back, you'd better have your head on straight." She crossed to her side of the room and pulled a small camcorder out from under her bed.

"Dry spell?" Ariana laughed.

"Not for long." Noelle smirked, heading for the door. She opened it and stepped into the hall. Billings was unusually quiet for a Sunday afternoon; most of the girls were probably still sleeping off hangovers from the night before.

"Oh, and Ariana?" Noelle called over her shoulder.

"Hmmm?" Ariana turned her head toward the door.

"Only an idiot would pass up a Daniel Ryan for a Thomas Pearson. That's obvious to the world, right?" Her dark eyes flashed.

Ariana's heart rose in her throat. She sat up quickly, banging her head on the headboard. "What? Noelle, I don't—"

But the slam of the door sliced through her voice. Ariana threw her pillow in frustration.

How did Noelle always know?

DISTANCE

"Something more, something more, something more," Ariana whispered to herself, staring up at the darkened ceiling from the comfort of her bed.

She hadn't moved in hours. Had just lain there obsessing about her unwritten paper. There was no way she was going to be able to sleep until she had some kind of breakthrough. Luckily, Noelle was still with Dash, so there was no one around to hear her talking to herself. Then, suddenly, her cell phone buzzed and she grabbed it, more than happy to let whoever was calling get her out of her head. The second she saw the name on the caller ID, her heart seized. It was already eleven o'clock. No good news came this late.

"Mom!" She sat up, propping a pillow behind her head. "Are you okay? What's wrong?"

"Hi, baby." On the other end of the line, her mom sounded far away, lost. Empty. "Just wanted to hear your voice, that's all. How's my angel?"

"I'm great, Mom. Fine." A lump rose in Ariana's throat even as relief washed through her. Her mom was okay. She sounded medicated, but okay. Ariana swallowed fiercely. "How are you? Where are you?"

"I'm still here, but I'm going home soon. I just signed all the paperwork a few minutes ago, so they should be letting me out in at least seventy-two hours." She laughed weakly. "Things take forever around here."

"I know, Mom." Ariana hated it when her mother called. She loved talking to her, loved telling her everything that was happening with classes and teachers and friends, but still, she hated the calls. Her mother always sounded so fragile, so weak, as if one wrong word, one wrong intonation, would break her. And Ariana knew—dreaded, really—that the time would come when she wouldn't be able to fix her anymore.

"So, sweet girl, tell me everything. How is Billings House?" For a brief moment, Ariana heard something in her mother's voice lift. She heard hope. Hope, and the sound of a doctor being paged in the background.

"Good, Mom. Really great." Ariana searched her mind for something to tell her mother that would make her happy. She had a feeling that her recent existential crisis concerning the loss of her virginity wasn't that something. "And things are going great with Daniel. We're leaving on Tuesday for Vermont."

"That's right!"

Ariana could hear the unfamiliar sound of a smile in her mother's voice. She rolled over to her side, glancing back at the photo of the two of them, and the tears surfaced again. The white Christmas lights around her window blurred together.

"The lodge where we're staying is supposed to be really incredible," Ariana said, letting a single tear slip down her cheek. "Apparently the vice president stays there every year." She couldn't believe she was regurgitating the same boring stories Daniel had lulled the entire table to sleep with the night before. But she knew that these stories were exactly the kinds of stories that her mother lived for.

"Oh, you're going to have such a fabulous time. Be sure to tell Daniel I said hello. And Dr. and Mrs. Ryan. Be sure to give them my best as well."

"I will, Mom." Ariana closed her eyes and forced her voice to stay steady. "But I'm going to miss coming home this year. Are you sure you don't want me to change my plans and fly down to Atlanta?"

"No, no," her mother said, too quickly. "Don't be ridiculous. You go with Daniel. I want you to go. You know I've always liked him so much." She paused. "I'm so proud of you, Ariana. So happy for you. You have everything I've always wanted you to have . . . everything I didn't get to have."

"I know. I just don't want you to be alone." Ariana bit her lip. "Promise you'll call me if you need anything? I don't know how great my cell service will be in the mountains, but—"

"Oh, for heaven's sake, Ariana, I'll be fine!" Her laugh was strained. There was a brief pause and the sound of muffled voices. "I have to get off the phone now," she said. "I'll talk to you soon, sweetheart."

"Okay. Love you, Mom. And congratulations on going home. Wish I could be there with you to celebrate."

"Love you too, baby."

Her eyes still closed, Ariana held the phone to her ear long after the line went dead.

DISCRETION

"How is it always colder in here than it is outside?" Ariana murmured as she followed Paige, Isobel, and Noelle through the arched doors of Easton's chapel the next morning. A shiver ran down her spine, and she tightened the sash on her white wool coat. Growing up in Georgia, she had never experienced the kind of cold that dominated the school year in Connecticut. It was a biting, relentless cold that seeped straight through to the bone and held on tight. No matter how many scarves and hats and coats Ariana acquired, she had yet to find a way to protect herself from it.

"I don't have time for this," Paige snapped. "My Louis Vuittons aren't going to pack themselves."

"Don't worry. It should be a short one," Isobel assured Paige, shaking out her glossy black hair after removing her wool slouch hat. "You'll be back to Louis before he has time to miss you."

Headmaster Cox had called the special morning assembly to

discuss campus protocol during winter break. Unlike Paige, Ariana was grateful for the distraction. She needed a break from looking at her blank laptop screen and worrying about her mom. Her mom, who would be home alone in just a matter of hours.

It was dark inside the chapel, thanks to the stained glass, which let in only a smidgen of the gray sky outside. The lamps that flickered around the lectern were the only sources of light in the room. Ariana hugged herself as she followed Noelle to the junior pews near the center of the chapel, parting ways with Isobel and Paige, who, as seniors and Billings Girls, took seats of privilege in the very last row. Easton was riddled with such small reminders of rank. Rituals that kept everything, everyone, in the appropriate place. Ariana slid into a seat next to two other Billings Girls in her class, Leanne Shore and Natasha Crenshaw, shooting them both a quick smile of greeting.

"Here. Take these," Noelle said, handing over her wool-and-cashmere gloves as Ariana blew on her hands. "Your fingers are turning purple."

"Thanks," Ariana said. She felt ten times better as she pulled the gloves on. It was nice, the way Noelle was always taking care of her. "All I want for Christmas is a good pair of gloves," she joked.

"I'll be sure to tell Daniel that. Nothing says romance like a big old pair of wool mittens." Noelle rolled her eyes.

"Attention, students." The chapel went deathly silent as Headmaster Cox spoke into the microphone at the lectern. His voice echoed around the chapel, bouncing from the rafters to the stained glass. "Welcome. My remarks will be brief, but they are important, and I suggest you pay close attention."

A loud snore sounded on the other side of the chapel, and Gage Coolidge slid down in his pew before any of the teachers had the chance to catch him. A few snickers rose up around him. Either Headmaster Cox didn't hear the boys' laughter, or he didn't care enough to acknowledge it. Ariana glanced across the aisle and saw Thomas giving Gage a silent high five. Mature. As always.

Seeing Thomas now in the light of day, messing around with Gage, Ariana was proud to realize that she felt absolutely nothing at all. No spark, no blush, no warmth. Perhaps it had just been the atmosphere, the few swallows of champagne she had indulged in. A moment of temporary insanity. Everyone had those, right?

"As you are all aware, Easton Academy's campus will be closed beginning at precisely six o'clock tomorrow evening," Headmaster Cox continued. Shadowy light from the lanterns played across the dean's partially bald head, almost as if a bunch of kids were making shadow puppets against it. "Six o'clock sharp. The only exceptions to this rule are the students who have already received my permission to be on campus. Those students, and those students alone, will stay in Drake for the duration of break. No other dormitories will be open to students during this time." Everyone knew that Headmaster Cox was talking about Easton's exchange students. They always stayed together over breaks and holidays, since it was usually too far for them to travel home. "The cost of heating each of the dormitories is too great, considering the relatively small number of students on campus."

"So all those thousands they extort from our parents for tuition can't pay the bills, huh?" Natasha whispered. She only briefly looked up from the *New York Times* crossword she was doing—in pen. Last month she'd announced that she was going to do this every day until she completed one all on her own.

"No luck yet?" Ariana whispered.

"Not for lack of working my ass off on it," Natasha joked in response, her dark eyes smiling as she filled in number twenty-four across. Then Leanne gave Ariana an unwarranted look of death and Ariana faced forward again. The two were roommates and best friends, but Ariana always thought that Leanne was a little bit too possessive when it came to Natasha.

Feeling frozen out of any further conversation, Ariana unwillingly let her mind drift back to the talk she'd had with her mother. Part of her was happy for her mom, happy that she could finally get away from the blank white walls, the cold nurses, and the restricted visiting hours. Happy that she could finally go home. But part of her knew that her mom wasn't ready. And Ariana couldn't go through it again. Couldn't come home to an eerily silent house. Couldn't call for her mother and hear the sound of her own voice echo in the soaring entrance hall. Couldn't run up the stairs, down the long hallway into the bedroom, and find—

"I repeat." Headmaster Cox's voice boomed throughout the chapel, and Ariana snapped to attention, her chest heaving, heart pounding. *No. Stop.* She had to stop torturing herself. It had been over two years ago, and still the images flashed in her mind as clearly as if it were

happening all over again. "Any student who is found to be in violation
of these rules will face immediate expulsion."

A fresh wave of silence swept over the student body. Headmaster
Cox was not one to make idle threats. Ariana willed herself to
breathe.

In . . . two . . . three . . .

Mom is fine. She's fine. She's going to be fine.

Out . . . two . . . three . . .

It's not going to happen again. You don't have to worry.

In . . . two . . . three . . .

It's over. It's all over. Just calm down. Calm . . .

From the corner of her eye, she caught Noelle glancing quizzically
in her direction. Ariana resumed a normal breathing cadence, but
she wasn't sure how long it would last. She needed air. Real air. It was
too cramped in these pews.

"This includes any student who is caught on campus without the
requisite paperwork, and any student who attempts to enter a dor-
mitory other than Drake," Headmaster Cox clarified. "There are no
exceptions. None." He paused for effect, gazing down with authority
at the students seated in front of him.

Suddenly Ariana saw the face of the EMT as clear as day. The one
who had been hovering over her when she awoke from shock.

I have to get out of here. Now.

"That is all. You are dismissed."

The noise level rose in the chapel before the headmaster had
the chance to step away from the microphone. Students crammed

together and rushed for the chapel doors, filling the center aisle. Dizziness overwhelmed Ariana as she jumped to her feet. She shoved past a group of sophomore girls and ignored Noelle's calls. She couldn't stop the thoughts of her mother, thoughts of that awful day, from flooding her mind, from suffocating her. Finally she reached the doors and stumbled under the archway, gulping in the sharp winter air. She leaned against the intricate stonework and closed her eyes, trying to distance herself from the students around her and her own thoughts, all at once. Trying to escape.

"Hey, naughty girl." A familiar voice oozing with confidence rose above the noise around her. She opened her eyes and saw Thomas standing in worn jeans and a thin gray T-shirt. Snowflakes fell around him, but he wore no coat. Nothing to guard against the weather except for a tattered brown cap. Still, he didn't seem to notice the cold.

Her heart flipped.

Dammit. So much for that. Apparently it had been the distance between them that had kept her body from reacting to him in the chapel.

"What?" Ariana asked, her face growing warm.

Thomas smirked. "I know you said you were a good girl, but that thigh-graze proved otherwise. Hence, the new name."

"I don't know what you're talking about." Ariana pursed her lips in disapproval, her voice low. "I was drunk. So I would appreciate it if you wouldn't call me that." She pushed away from the wall and headed around the side of the chapel toward the academic buildings.

"Like you don't *love* the idea of me having a special name for you," Thomas said, following after her.

Ariana whirled on him. "I don't. Just leave me alone," she snapped.

Thomas held up his hands for a brief moment, but then fell into step with her, a maddening grin spreading over his face. "I don't think you were drunk. And I don't think it was a mistake." Against the backdrop of the heavy gray skies, his blue eyes seemed to glow. He pushed back the long bangs that spilled over his forehead.

Ariana looked away, fixing her gaze straight ahead. "It doesn't matter what you think," she said in what she hoped was a light tone.

"Whatever you have to tell yourself." Thomas laughed.

Ariana shook her head, as if she could erase the memory of what she'd done on Saturday night like an Etch A Sketch. Her mom's fragile voice echoed in her mind, her excitement about Daniel. About the Ryans. All Ariana wanted was to forget about Saturday evening. Forget about Daniel's stupid drunkenness. Forget the way Thomas had made her feel free. Forget the way Thomas had looked at her, like he knew what she was thinking. He didn't. No one did. Not Daniel. Not even Noelle. And definitely not Thomas.

She paused in the center of the quad and turned to Thomas, leveling him with the most serious glare she could muster.

"Let me say it again. Slowly so that you can understand through the haze of whatever drugs you're currently road-testing. Leave. Me. Alone."

Thomas's face fell. For a split second he actually looked hurt. But then, just as quickly, he regained his cocky composure.

"Fine. I'll leave you alone. For now." He glanced left, smiled, then looked back at her. "Later, naughty girl."

As soon as he was gone, Ariana glanced over to see what had made him smile and her stomach clenched. She found herself face-to-face with Daniel and Paige.

Ariana's fingers shook and she gripped her left forearm with her right hand, practically cutting off her own circulation even through her heavy coat. Had they been behind her the whole time? Had they heard her conversation with Thomas? She forced a smile, leaning in to give Daniel a peck on the cheek.

"I didn't know you guys were there."

Had they heard him call her naughty girl? If so, her life as she knew it was over.

"Obviously." Paige's smile was frozen on her face, her eyes cold. "Ready for class?"

Ariana nodded, afraid to speak.

"Good." Paige stepped between Daniel and Ariana. "Then let's go."

"See you later," Daniel said. His expression was confused, but not hurt. Not angry. Ariana had no idea what to think.

"Yeah. Later."

Ariana and Paige started across the quad and Ariana's every step was shaky, tentative, as she waited for Paige's attack—but it never came. Not in words, anyway. But every once in a while Ariana could almost feel Paige's cold, judging stare boring into the side of her face. She refused to look over and meet her eyes. Instead, she told herself over and over that it was just her imagination.

And she almost believed it.

C'EST MOI

"You've all heard the saying 'Life imitates art'? Well, this was a perfect example." Mr. Holmes leaned against the mahogany desk at the front of the classroom, his copy of *Madame Bovary* in one hand and a stainless steel coffee mug in the other. "When Flaubert's story of an unhappy, unfaithful married woman was printed in the *Revue de Paris*, Flaubert himself was brought to trial on charges of immorality."

"He's so hot when he's talking about immorality," Paige whispered from the chair next to Ariana's.

"Agreed," Isobel said. "Almost makes me want to read the thing." She tossed her glossy black tresses over her shoulder. "Almost."

Ariana rolled her eyes and focused on taking notes. Almost every girl on campus had a crush on the young English teacher, who had come to Easton several years ago after graduating from Princeton. But Ariana didn't care about his looks. She loved the way he made the characters, the worlds they read about, come alive. Being invited to be a part of his Topics in Eighteenth-Century French Literature seminar was a huge honor. There were only eight people in the class, all seniors, with the exception of her. She loved that Mr. Holmes thought she was smart enough—good enough—for one of the toughest classes at Easton.

"The thing is, Flaubert did feel a real connection with Emma Bovary," Mr. Holmes was saying. "He wrote many of his own personal flaws into her character. One of his most famous quotes is '*Madame Bovary, c'est moi.*'" He rolled up the sleeves of his crisp white collared shirt. "Translation?"

"What is, 'I am Madame Bovary'?" blurted Connie Tolson, a nerdy senior seated a few chairs to Ariana's right. Her ramrod-straight posture made her look like she had just pulled something in one of the major muscle groups.

Mr. Holmes chuckled. "Absolutely right, Ms. Tolson. Bonus points for the creative delivery." He dropped the book on his desk and wiped his palms on his khakis, leaving faint chalk stains.

"Oh, please. What is, 'desperate and so out of her league'?" Isobel hissed, a wry grin creasing her olive cheek.

Ariana shook her head. "You're terrible."

Isobel smiled. "And proud of it."

"Remarkably, Flaubert establishes a strong connection between his readers and Emma. So even though she's weaving a web of excess, sex, and betrayal, we really empathize with Emma throughout the novel," Mr. Holmes continued. "We see the destruction this woman is causing, solely for the purpose of her own fulfillment, and still we feel for her. In a strange way, we root for her, want her to find happiness. And we're devastated when she doesn't."

"Um, I'm not," Connie called out. "She was wrong to cheat on her husband so many times. A woman who does things like that doesn't deserve to be happy."

And a girl who wore red slip-on ankle boots didn't deserve to be a student at Easton, but Ariana wasn't raising her hand and announcing it to the class. She kept her eyes on Connie, taking in the holier-than-thou smirk she was broadcasting in hi-def around the semicircle.

"Interesting idea, Miss Tolson." Mr. Holmes raised an eyebrow. "But I'll play the devil's advocate here. Don't we all deserve to be happy? Or at least to search for what we think might make us happy? Isn't that a basic human right?"

"Not if being happy means you're hurting someone else," Connie replied matter-of-factly.

"I agree," Paige announced. Shock passed over Connie's pinched features, and Isobel nearly choked on her coffee. "People who don't think about how their actions affect the people they love are selfish." She leaned forward in her chair, looking past Isobel and directly at Ariana. "Don't you think, Ariana?" she asked sweetly. Her green eyes blazed.

Ariana's pulse raced. Paige had heard Thomas's nickname for her. There was no other explanation.

"Miss Osgood? Care to weigh in on this one?" Mr. Holmes smiled.

"Actually, I do," she said quietly, taking a deep breath. If they had been inside Billings, Ariana would probably have submitted to being bullied by Paige, but not here. Not where it might affect her grade. "I don't think it's fair to place all of the responsibility for Charles Bovary's happiness on Emma. He's responsible for his own happiness, just like she's responsible for hers." Mr. Holmes nodded, and Ariana felt her voice strengthening. "And even though she never found it, at least she had the guts to try."

Connie crossed her arms over her navy sweater vest and flashed a judgmental glare. "So you're saying it's okay to have . . ." She paused, tossing her skinny French braid over her shoulder. ". . . *intercourse* with as many people as you want to, just to make yourself happy?"

"Sounds like Emma isn't the one who needs to be having intercourse," Isobel said, just loudly enough. Ariana could have sworn she saw a hint of a smile pass over Mr. Holmes's face.

She'd known she liked him.

"That's not what I'm saying." Ariana shook her head emphatically, avoiding Paige's glare. "She made mistakes, and she paid for them. We all make mistakes, and I think that's what makes us feel so close to Emma. She's human. She's flawed. But she's doing her best, and we have to give her some credit for that." She sank back into her chair, surprised at the tirade that had slipped, almost involuntarily, from her lips. She hadn't known she felt so strongly about the issue until she was face-to-face with Connie and Paige and their intolerant views. But she was smart enough to know why she had reacted the way she had.

Thomas.

"Ariana's absolutely right," Mr. Holmes said, slipping his book into a leather messenger bag on top of his desk. "Emma Bovary's flaws are what make her so accessible to us. And she does pay for her mistakes. Although, Miss Osgood," he said kindly, "one could also argue that her painful death is retribution for her immoral behavior."

Ariana felt a distinct pang in her chest. Like Holmes was condemning her to the same fate as Emma Bovary right then and there.

"Like karma," Ariana said quietly.

"Exactly like karma," Mr. Holmes replied, fiddling with his wedding band. He glanced up at the clock. "Sorry, folks. I kept you a few minutes late. We'll continue this discussion after the break, so if you have any thoughts on morality as it relates to the book, jot them down and bring them in." He pulled a folded newspaper from his back pocket. Like Natasha, Mr. Holmes was always working on the *New York Times* crossword puzzle. "Just a reminder that your papers are due *in my mailbox*—no e-mail attachments, people—before you leave campus," he called over the din of chatting students. "Have a great break, everyone."

The paper. Suddenly, Ariana's blood coursed through her veins at a fevered rate. In all the morning's drama, she had completely forgotten about the paper. And so far, all she had was a blank Word document and a massive case of writer's block—which was unlike her. Ariana had always been able to focus, no matter what was happening around her. As a child, she'd learned to sink into her own mind and settle there until it was safe to return to reality. To curl up in bed with *Jane Eyre* or *Mrs. Dalloway* and pretend she didn't hear the chilling screams, the threats her mother tossed at her father like active grenades. *Just try me. I'll do it. . . . I swear to God, I'll do it, and you'll be sorry. . . .*

"What's wrong with you?" Isobel pulled a pair of oversize Gucci sunglasses from her tote and slipped them on as Ariana and Paige gathered their things.

"Nothing," Ariana said, nervous about making eye contact with Paige. Paige had the power to make her winter break miserable. To make her life in Billings miserable. In her quest to please Mr. Holmes, she had gone temporarily insane and forgotten that fact. Why had she felt the need to show Paige up? No one crossed Paige Ryan, and everyone at Easton knew that. Even Connie Tolson. "It's just this paper," she told Isobel as she buttoned her coat. "I'm nowhere close to being done. I think I'm going to have to stay behind for a day or so to finish."

"That's ridiculous," Paige scoffed. "Just ask for an extension."

Isobel nodded. "He let me turn in my paper on *Dangerous Liaisons* a week late."

"Yeah. I suppose," Ariana said, even though the thought filled her throat with bile. She had never asked for an extension before, and she didn't want to start now. But she knew that Paige wasn't simply suggesting that Ariana get an extension. Paige didn't suggest. She ordered. Clearly the idea of Ariana missing a day of Daniel's precious Christmas plans was unacceptable to her. "I'll ask," Ariana conceded, letting her blond hair fall over her face as she reached down to pick up her bag. Anything to avoid having to look at Paige. "I'll catch up with you guys later."

"Later," Isobel said lightly. Ariana watched as she and Paige sashayed past Mr. Holmes's desk and out the door. She sat quietly in her chair as the classroom emptied, her insides writhing with nerves. She hated the idea of asking for more time, of losing Mr. Holmes's respect. But short of pissing Paige off even more than she already had, it was her only option.

"Mr. Holmes?" Ariana's voice sounded small. She cleared her throat and tried again. "Can I ask you a question?"

Mr. Holmes looked up from his crossword puzzle. "Of course, Miss Osgood," he smiled. "What can I do for you?"

He had a way of making her feel calm, self-assured. She took a deep breath. "I was just wondering if I could get an extension on the paper? I'm leaving town tomorrow morning with my boyfriend, and—" She stopped, her face flushing. Why had she mentioned Daniel? A completely unnecessary detail, and not one that made her case any stronger. Her heart felt like lead in her chest as she saw Mr. Holmes slowly shaking his head.

"I'm afraid not," he said, interlacing his ink-stained hands on the desk in front of him. "Ordinarily, I would, but I have to get final grades in to the registrar by Friday at noon. I'm sorry."

Ariana's heart sank. "Right. Okay. Thanks anyway."

She quickly rose from her chair and slipped out of the classroom before Mr. Holmes could say another word. Her face burned with humiliation. She knew she shouldn't have asked. It was a mistake. A mistake that she would now have to remedy by writing an A+ paper, since he was now going to be expecting something substandard. And she was going to have to pull this A+ paper out of thin air in a matter of hours. Otherwise, she was going to be forced to explain to Paige why she couldn't leave for Vermont tomorrow. And facing Paige was the last thing she wanted to do.

NOT FRIENDS

"Would you just pick something so we can get out of here?" Noelle snapped as she stood between two racks of windbreakers in downtown Easton's North Face store. With her flawless skin, Tiffany diamonds sparkling in her ears, and a Longchamp tote hanging from the crook of her arm, she looked like a mannequin that had accidentally been displayed in the wrong store.

"Okay, what about this?" Ariana held up a ski hat—red, fleece, thermal.

"Really? We've been standing in this hot-as-hell store for half an hour so you can buy him fleece?" Noelle said. "I don't understand. You already bought him a perfectly acceptable Christmas present."

"I just wanted to get him something a little extra," Ariana said, feeling deflated.

"Then just get the hat and let's go. This place is giving me hives," Noelle said, adjusting her scarf.

"I don't know. . . ."

Noelle groaned and slipped her sunglasses on. "Whatever. Come meet me at Sweet Nothings when you're done being obsessive."

"I'm not being obsessive," Ariana replied. But Noelle was already gone, filling the store with cold air as she swept out. "I'm not," Ariana repeated quietly to herself as she fingered the red hat.

But of course she was. The second she'd left Mr. Holmes's class, she'd felt this overwhelming *need* to buy Daniel the perfect pre-Christmas gift. True, she'd already gotten him a Tag Heuer watch engraved with his initials. But after her conversation with Paige, she realized that she needed to do something to prove her devotion to Daniel. And that something couldn't wait until Christmas Day.

But now it was five fifty-five. She still hadn't started her paper, and the store was closing in five minutes. Ariana wanted more than anything to follow Noelle, to just leave, but she couldn't walk away. She had gotten it into her mind that she needed something more for Daniel, and she couldn't go back to Billings until she had found something.

One of the salesgirls started cashing out her register while the beefy manager hung around by the door, his keys already out. Ariana suddenly felt stretched tight and panicky. Why had she convinced herself that the only thing that could bring her back to center was a stupid hat? Picking up a thick cashmere scarf, Ariana decided not to dwell on the nagging suspicion that it was because being worthy of Daniel went—in Paige's mind, at least—hand in hand with being worthy of Billings. And the idea that Paige might have heard Ariana and Thomas talking after morning assembly made Ariana sick to her stomach. But there was no way to be sure exactly what Paige knew, or what she suspected—and Paige would never come right out and say it. That would be too easy. A cryptic comment here, an icy stare there, until Ariana went insane. Slow, murderous torture. That was the Billings way.

She sighed, put the scarf down, and examined the sleeve of a blue windbreaker. Suddenly a frigid hand clamped the back of her neck and Ariana's breath caught in her throat. She whirled around. Thomas Pearson smirked down at her. Even as her heart stopped beating and her neck tingled where he'd touched her, she forced her eyes to narrow in indignation.

"What is your problem?" she snapped.

"You shouldn't scare so easy," he replied with his irritatingly sexy smirk. A light dusting of snowflakes was scattered over his hair, and his nose and cheeks were flushed, his eyes bright. Adrenaline raced through Ariana's veins, making her entire body feel shaky.

"What are you doing here?" She glanced quickly around. Apart from the salesgirl and the manager, there were only two other people in the store, both girls, but neither from Easton Academy.

"Um, shopping?" He looked at her like she'd lost her mind.

"Like you'd ever wear North Face," she replied, hoping her pounding heart wasn't visible through her sweater. "Aren't you more of a grunge boy than a ski rat?"

"So now you're keeping tabs on my style?" Thomas raised an eyebrow.

"Stop doing that," she demanded, trying to keep her voice low. She fought the urge to fan her cheeks. Had it been this hot in here just two minutes ago?

"Doing what?" he smirked.

"Acting like you know me. Like we're friends." Thick tension hovered in the space between them. God, she wanted to reach out and brush the snow out of his hair. Instead she turned away from him for a moment and grabbed the red hat up again. "We're not."

"No kidding."

He took a step closer to her. So close she could see that the blue right around his pupils was slightly darker than the rest of his eyes. Her heart thudded in her chest and her breath came out short and raspy. Because even though she was holding the hat she was about to buy for Daniel, she wanted to pull it over Thomas's dark hair and pull his lips to hers. She wasn't supposed to be attracted to someone like Thomas, someone who didn't make sense, someone who could make her lose control, someone who was right now leaning in to *kiss her.*

She closed her eyes, feeling his warm breath, waiting for the contact.

Suddenly, the clothing rack behind them jarred, sending Ariana tumbling forward into Thomas's chest.

"Oops!" A girl's voice sounded on the other side of the rack. "Sorry."

Heart pounding, Ariana pushed away from Thomas, her eyes darting around the back of the store. The walls were getting closer, pressing the racks of thick clothing in all around her, squeezing out the air. She felt as if her ribs were curling in on her chest, crushing her lungs. Her temples pulsed.

"You need to leave. Now."

"Ariana. What's wrong?"

Even in the midst of her growing panic, she heard the concern in his usually playful voice and was touched. She braced a hand on top of a metal rack full of ski jackets and forced herself to breathe.

In . . . two . . . three . . .

Out . . . two . . . three. . . .

"Are you okay?"

He touched her back with his palm and she flinched away. Of course she wasn't okay. She was in the middle of a panic attack. Couldn't he see that? She had been careless, had let her guard down for just a second. Had done it where anyone could see. It was too dangerous. If word ever got back to Paige . . . Ariana didn't want to think about what could happen. What Paige had the power to do. Things had almost gone too far. That could not happen again. Ever.

"Just go," she said, her voice raspy.

"Fine." And just like that, the concern was gone. His face shut down. And then he was gone as well.

Ariana closed her eyes and continued to count through her breathing. In . . . two . . . three . . . Out, two, three. Until the walls finally expanded again. Until the air whooshed back and her skin began to cool. When she opened her eyes again, the remaining salesgirl was eyeing her warily from the counter.

"We're closing," the girl said with disdain. As if she were talking to some smelly street urchin who had come in solely to loiter and get warm.

Move, Ariana told herself. *Just move.*

She lifted her chin and somehow made it to the front of the store, where she paid for Daniel's hat. She no longer cared if it was perfect. She just needed to buy it and get the hell out of there. She needed to get back to Billings. Better yet, she needed to get away, period. As she exited into the night, she barely felt the icy wind whip her hair around her face.

"What exactly were you doing in there?" Noelle hooked her arm through Ariana's and nodded toward the front of the North Face store.

Ariana's blood ran cold. Why wasn't Noelle in Sweet Nothings? Why was she waiting for her on the street? Had she seen Thomas leave? But following Noelle's gaze, Ariana realized Noelle was pointing at Sergei, who was strolling across the street, a small North Face shopping bag swinging from his wrist. He must have walked out right before Ariana had. How had she not noticed him inside?

"Looks like your little Latvian admirer has upgraded to stalker." Noelle smirked. She gave Sergei a mocking little wave. He stuffed his hands in his pockets and upped his pace. "How cute," she said sardonically.

"Noelle, that is *not* cute. I cannot have a stalker."

Especially not if he saw me with Thomas. Ariana clenched her fists as Sergei glanced back at her with his cold, flat eyes. Had he been in the store the whole time? Had he witnessed her panic attack? And—even worse—had he seen what she and Thomas had almost done? Ariana's pulse started racing again.

"Oh, please. He's totally harmless," Noelle said with a dismissive flick of the wrist. "So he has a little crush. Who the hell cares?"

I do, Ariana thought as Noelle dragged her down the sidewalk. Because if Sergei had seen her with Thomas—had seen them almost kiss—then she cared *very* much.

INVITE

"What do you mean you can't leave for Vermont?" Daniel's eyes blazed.

Morning light poured through the large windows on the far side of Easton's dining hall. As the room started to fill with students, the sounds of laughter, clinking silverware, and scraping chairs bubbled up around Ariana. She shifted in her wooden seat, glancing around to see if anyone was watching. Of course, they were. But luckily, most of the Billings Girls had yet to arrive.

"It's just that I have to finish this paper," she said quietly.

Or, more accurately, *start* this paper. Ariana had stayed up all night trying to put her thoughts on paper, but unfortunately the only thoughts in her mind were about sex. She kept trying to picture losing her virginity to Daniel, kept trying to map it out in her mind so she'd be prepared when it happened. All night long she had been imagining her and Daniel in the posh lodge bedroom with candles all around.

She was wearing her favorite white silk nightgown; he was wearing a T-shirt and striped pajama pants. He started to kiss her. They slowly undressed. The whole thing was fine. Perfect even. But then, when she arrived at the pivotal moment in her daydream, Daniel always morphed into Thomas. Every time. And then she would break out in a sweat and have to start the whole thing over again.

At this rate, she was never going to be prepared. And she was never going to write that paper, either.

"How long have you known this was going to happen?" Daniel demanded.

"Since last night," Ariana admitted.

Daniel huffed an exaggerated sigh. "Then why didn't you call me?"

Because I couldn't bear to let you down, Ariana thought. *I couldn't admit that I'd failed. Failed you, failed us, failed . . . failed . . . failed. . . .*

"I don't know," she said lamely.

"Ari, the Hearsts are coming over for dinner tonight. I wanted you to be there. My parents are *expecting* you to be there." A vein along Daniel's temple pulsed.

Ariana grabbed her forearm and squeezed. She hated when Daniel got like this. It made her feel so small. "I know, and I'm sorry. I just need this afternoon, and then I'll come up and join you. I just can't leave with you in an hour."

"This freakin' sucks."

"I know. But I got you a present to keep you warm until I get there," she said with false enthusiasm, handing him a silver-wrapped box with a red velvet ribbon. She had spent forty-five minutes getting the bow just right.

Daniel just looked at it, still stewing.

"Open it!" Ariana said brightly.

He sighed again and tore the ribbon off, letting it fall to the floor. Ariana watched it flutter to the floor, her jaw clenched in irritation.

It was just a bow, she told herself. *You can't expect a guy to notice a bow....*

Daniel pulled the hat out and stared at it, saying nothing. The seconds felt like hours. She wished he would accept her apology and move on. The dining hall was filling up quickly now, and the Billings Girls were almost through the line. She didn't want to have this conversation in front of everyone. Especially not Paige.

"Daniel?" Ariana prompted.

"It's great. Thanks," he said moodily. He tossed the box on the table just as their friends started to arrive.

"Uh-oh. Someone's pissed," Noelle teased Daniel. She placed her tray of cereal and fruit down and sank into her usual spot next to Ariana. Paige, Dash, and Isobel filled the other seats. "Did Ari tell you about her hot rendezvous last night?" It was as if all the air had been drained from the cafeteria. As everyone turned to look at her, Ariana clutched her coffee mug so tightly her knuckles turned white. Noelle couldn't be talking about Thomas, right? Had she seen them after all?

"Don't bother playing coy," Paige said, sitting down at the head of the table and biting into a green apple. Her face looked pinched. Angry. "It's insulting."

"Yeah." Isobel smiled. "Noelle already told us all about your Latvian *lovah*," she said, licking a dollop of yogurt from the back of her spoon.

"Your Latvian lover?" Daniel looked baffled.

"You know, *Sergei*," Noelle sang, brushing her dark hair over her shoulder.

The entire table dissolved into laughter, and Ariana felt all the tension flow out of her body. She forced a laugh and counted the number of buttons on Noelle's Marc Jacobs blouse—twelve—until her heart settled in her chest.

"That freak? What'd he do now?" Daniel snapped.

"Nothing," Ariana replied. "We just happened to be in the same store at the same time."

The explanation seemed to satisfy Daniel. He picked a grape out of Ariana's fruit cup and slumped back in his chair, brooding as he chewed. Clearly he was still annoyed about Ariana's announcement, but at least he knew nothing about Thomas.

"So what time are you leaving, Noelle?" Isobel asked.

Ariana buttered her toast and let the conversation wash over her. She noticed Thomas sitting a few tables over, shaking his head at Gage, who was doubled over in laughter. A few tables down from them was Sergei sitting alone, wearing his trademark argyle sweater and glasses, hunched over a book. Ariana didn't know why the sight of him make her heart ping in her chest. She shouldn't feel sorry for him. He was creepy and possibly stalking her. But she couldn't help but feel like she understood him a little. Because even though she had friends, had Billings, she could relate to his loneliness. No one really knew her, either.

Daniel touched her arm. Swallowing the gigantic lump that was now hovering in her throat, Ariana tuned back into the conversation. When she looked into his eyes, she could see that he'd decided to forgive her. She felt her shoulders relax.

"Is there anything I can do?" he offered, smoothing his green khakis over his knees. "Make it easier for you to get out of here on time?"

"Like what?" Ariana asked as Paige speared a piece of grapefruit with a butter knife. An acidic drop landed on Ariana's cheek. Paige smirked a halfhearted apology and went back to her grapefruit.

"Write a few pages while you pack?" Daniel offered.

"You haven't even read the book!" Ariana laughed.

"Doesn't matter," Dash said over a mouthful of bagel. "Dude can pull any assignment out of his ass. He wrote Gage's Western civ term paper in an hour and a half last year and he got an A-minus."

Ariana glanced quizzically at Daniel, and he shrugged. "Lost a bet," he explained.

"Thanks," Ariana smiled, happy that, for the moment, things seemed back to normal. "But I have to finish this on my own. If you want to help, you can take my bags up to Vermont so I don't have to deal with them on the train."

"You got it. Anything else?"

"You can try on your present," she said playfully.

She grabbed the fleece hat off the table and tugged it over his head.

Daniel pulled that hat down over his eyes, then pushed it up again so that it was just above his brow. He smiled adorably at Ariana.

"What do you think?" he asked.

"Very sexy," she replied with a laugh.

Noelle rolled her eyes and took a sip of her coffee.

Daniel tugged the hat off and stuffed it in his backpack. "I love it. Thanks. Really."

"You're—" The sound of Ariana's cell vibrating on the table cut her off. It buzzed loudly, vibrating slowly across the table. Isobel and Paige watched as Ariana reached out and picked it up. The blue screen flashed the words 1 NEW TXT MSG. She flipped the phone open, curious. Everyone who would text her was sitting right here.

Old chapel, 7 p.m. Don't be late, naughty girl.

Her heart stopped and she glanced up. Thomas was still sitting with Gage just a few tables away. But this time, he was looking directly at her. She blushed and immediately snapped the phone shut.

"Who's that?" Daniel was looking at her curiously. She forced herself to look back.

"Hmmm?" she asked, still gripping the phone in her hand.

"On the phone," Daniel said impatiently. He reached for her cell, but Ariana stuffed it into her Kate Spade bag, hoping Daniel couldn't see her clenched jaw, the nervous energy that was now racing through her.

"Nobody," she said quickly.

"What's the matter with you?" Daniel demanded, his shoulders rigid and angry. "Why won't you let me see it?"

"Why won't you let me have any privacy?" Ariana shot back. Her face burned. Isobel, Dash, Noelle, and Paige had all abandoned their breakfasts to watch their argument.

Daniel's eyes flashed. "Because. You're my girlfriend."

"Wow. Medieval much, Daniel?" Noelle joked.

Ariana could have hugged her friend for standing up for her.

"He's right," Paige said in a tone that dared any of them to contradict her. "He does have a right to know. Especially when she's acting so cagey."

Noelle looked down at her food, rolling her eyes only slightly.

"I'm not being cagey," Ariana said steadily, willing herself to not sound defensive.

"So who was it, Ariana?" Paige challenged.

"Fine! It was my mother, okay? She texts me these sappy messages and they're too embarrassing to show to anyone," Ariana improvised, hoping they couldn't see through her. Couldn't see the red LIAR sign that had to be flashing over her head. "Can the inquisition end now?"

"Your mom knows how to text?" Paige asked, looking skeptical. The clasp on her citrine-and-diamond necklace had fallen to the front, and she quickly adjusted the chain.

"She's on Instant Messenger, too. It's bizarre." Ariana shrugged, trying to appear blithe. But as desperate as she was for everyone to believe her, she started to feel anger burn at her core. She had *never* done anything wrong before. Never given Daniel reason to worry. And maybe she had made one small—teeny, really—misstep with Thomas, but she was always so *good*.

Noelle yawned. "That's it," she announced. "I'm officially bored." She got up and pulled on her camel-colored suede coat over her cardigan. "I've got to finish packing."

"Same." Dash nodded.

"And I need to finish my paper." Ariana stood up and grabbed her bag, swinging it over her left shoulder, away from Paige. Just in case the girl made a swipe for her phone. Glancing across the room, she saw that Thomas was looking at her again, watching intently. "See you later?" she said to Daniel.

"I'll come by to get your stuff," he said, rising to give her a quick kiss.

Keeping her eyes on Thomas, Ariana pulled Daniel closer and turned his peck into a long, deep kiss. By the time she was done, Daniel was blushing and Thomas looked stunned. As Ariana turned and walked with Noelle toward the exit, she couldn't help smiling.

Maybe Thomas was right. Maybe she was a little naughty after all.

CARELESS

A razor-thin sliver of dusk glowed outside Ariana's window, the last remnant of day before darkness enveloped the campus. She checked her watch. It was exactly 6 p.m. on Tuesday. She had one hour to put her paper in Mr. Holmes's mailbox and catch a cab to the train station.

As she leaned over her desk and clicked the print command on her laptop, her eyes fell on the framed photo perched on her desk, the one next to the picture of her and her mom. It was the black-and-white shot Daniel had taken of her. Ariana was wrapped in a fluffy, oversize beach towel and stretched out on a lounge chair, blowing a kiss to the camera. The girl in that picture looked happy. In love with her boyfriend. Normal.

She could be that girl again. She wanted to be. Thomas might be sexy and exciting, but Daniel was familiar. She knew everything about him. No surprises. For better or worse, he was the guy for her. The guy who could give her everything she wanted. Everything her mother wanted. Thomas was just a blip.

She pulled her cell phone from her Kate Spade tote, scrolled through her text messages, and read Thomas's one last time. Then she deleted it. As soon as the text was gone, she felt better. Lighter, somehow. She'd made her decision.

She snatched her paper from the printer tray, stapled it hastily together, and stuffed it in her bag. Winding a soft aqua scarf around her neck, she glanced one last time at the photographs on her desk. She'd made the right decision. The decision her mom would approve of. She slung her bag over her shoulder and slipped out of the room without looking back.

A lacy curtain of snow draped over her the moment she stepped outside Billings House. As she cut across the deserted grounds, the snow seemed to be falling heavier, thicker around her than it had earlier in the day. Hell Hall loomed just ahead, dark and imposing against the snowy sky. She took the stairs two at a time, and pushed through the doorway.

The lights had already been turned off. The sound of her footsteps echoed down the hall as she hurried in the dark to the faculty mail-room. She slid her hands along the wall and paused when she reached the last door. She strained to hear the sound of a professor's laugh, or a muffled conversation. Nothing but thick silence buzzing loudly in her ears.

She leaned against the heavy, stubborn door, nudging it with her hip to force it open. A dusty Tiffany lamp glowed on a table in the far corner of the room. Rows of small wooden cubbies stretched along one wall, and she scanned the names below each mailbox until she found Mr. Holmes's slot. She pulled her paper from her bag and stood on tiptoe, sliding it into his already overstuffed cubby.

A loud clatter in the hallway shattered the silence, and Ariana instinctively ducked behind the wall of mailboxes. She had thought she was alone. Immediately she felt silly. Easton was the safest place in the world. She just wasn't used to the place being empty. Shaking her head, she was about to come out when she heard footsteps, and something told her to stay where she was. She heard a door opening—or was it was the wind rattling the ancient windows? She couldn't tell. She held her breath and closed her eyes. Silence.

What was going on? The campus was practically deserted. Who else would be coming to Hell Hall at this hour? Slowly, Ariana pulled open the door and stepped cautiously into the hallway. It was empty. She quickly headed for the door but felt the overwhelming sensation that someone was watching her. Her steps turned into a jog, and the only sound she could hear was her heart pounding loudly in her ears.

This is stupid, she chided herself even as she ran. *There's no one here. No one. No one. No—*

Just a few feet from the double doors, she slammed into something. Someone. Ariana screamed. A hand clamped over her mouth and her back slammed into the wall. A hooded figure. Strong and tall, but thin. Ariana opened her mouth to bite down when she caught the familiar, spicy scent of Thomas Pearson.

"Calm down! It's just me."

He let her go and she gulped in a huge breath.

"Jesus, Thomas. Do you have a death wish or something?" Ariana sank back against the wall, adrenaline draining from her body. She wiped her clammy hands on her coat and tried to slow her breathing. "What the hell are you doing here?"

"Just in the neighborhood." He lowered his hood and laughed. She felt her body begin to relax. Even in the dimly lit hall, his eyes were stunningly blue.

"Try again." She felt the heat radiating from his body. She knew it was ridiculous, but suddenly she felt warmer.

"Okay. I knew you would need a little help getting to the chapel."

Ariana's heart skipped a beat, but she remembered her decision. She had to stick to her plan. "I can't. I have to catch a cab. I'm meeting Daniel in Vermont tonight."

"So go in the morning," he said simply, moving closer.

She took a step back, bumping in to the hallway wall. He was mere inches from her now, and Ariana felt the resistance melting from her body. It was as if he had some sort of power over her. The power to make her forget what she had with Daniel. To forget what could happen if anyone saw her with him. What she could lose. Billings. Easton. Her mother.

But when he was that close, all that existed was Thomas. All that she wanted was Thomas.

"You know you want to stay." He took another step closer. The tips of his shoes bumping against hers.

I do, Ariana thought, her longing taking over. *I do, I do, do.*

She had to touch him. Had to kiss him. Now. Right now or she was going to lose her mind.

"Aria—"

She silenced him with her touch. She grabbed him around the back of his neck and pulled his mouth down on hers. Power surged through her body as she took control, kissing him until he finally woke up from his shock and kissed her back. He yanked her scarf from around her neck, and his lips moved down from just below her ear, down, down to her collarbone. He groped for the buttons on her coat as she struggled with the belt. The moment she was free of it, his hand slipped inside and under her sweater. Her skin seared everywhere he touched her. She let the coat drop to the floor and slid her hands up under his clothes, running her fingers over his chest. Every inch of her body trembled with excitement, with a kind of energy she'd never felt before. Want flooded through her and she gave in to it, feeling completely, wonderfully out of control. She needed more. More. More *now*.

But when he starting pulling her sweater over her head, she pushed him away. "Wait. Not here," she whispered. "The professors . . . they're still around. . . ."

Wordlessly, he grabbed her hand. Ariana had just enough time to grab her coat and bag off the marble floor as he tugged her toward the double doors. Once outside, the snowflakes swirled thick around them, and Ariana felt as if her heart were swirling too. Wildly spinning with no chance of stopping. She didn't think about how she was supposed to be in love with Daniel. How she was supposed to be on her way to the train station. She just let Thomas lead her through campus to the edge of the woods. She had no idea what was going to happen. How far she would let things go.

And for the first time in her life, she didn't care.

DESTROYED

"After you." Thomas held back several thick, snow-covered pine branches. Behind them were a series of cracked stone steps leading to the old chapel's doorway. The building had been marked for demolition at the beginning of the year and was supposed to be torn down by the end of December. The student body had been warned by Dean Marcus to stay away from the woods until the area was cleared, but a select few, Thomas included, had ignored the dean's warning. It was the perfect place to drink and get high.

"I haven't been back here in a while." Ariana tilted her head back, taking in the circular stained-glass window above the door and the crumbling steeple that stretched into the cloud of snow above. She felt a sudden, unexpected surge of sadness. The old building had withstood so much over the years and had become strangely more beautiful, stronger with age. But it was only a matter of time before it would be completely destroyed. Gone forever.

Thomas made his way up the steps and pushed the door opened with a creak, gesturing for Ariana to go inside. She took a deep breath and crossed the threshold.

"Shit, it's freezing," he whispered as he closed the door behind them. His breath hovered white and heavy in the stale air.

Ariana nodded silently, even though she knew he couldn't see her in the dark. She braced herself against the bitter cold that permeated her clothes, seeping into her skin and chilling her insides. With any luck it would keep her brain frozen so she wouldn't have to think about what she was doing. That she was in a condemned chapel. With Thomas. Alone.

"Here we go." A flash of light exploded in front of Thomas, and he lowered his lighter to two candles in wall sconces on either side of the door. The dim light cast shadows over the rows of dusty pews and cracked stained-glass windows that ran the length of the small chapel. "Hey, can you light those?" Thomas handed her the lighter and nodded toward the altar.

Ariana took the lighter gingerly and held it in front of her, making her way slowly to the altar. The flame caught on a shard of blue glass at her feet. She knelt to pick it up, suddenly overwhelmed by the decaying beauty around her. This place was cracked and broken, just like she was. She felt the weight, the gravity of the space. Of all who had been there before. She could sense the ghosts all around her, spirits of students long dead and forgotten, clinging to the hallowed walls of their glory days.

One day, that would be her. And Thomas. And Noelle and

Daniel and Isobel and the rest. One day they would all be dead and gone. . . .

"Ariana?"

Thomas's voice jolted her. The metal of the lighter burned her thumb and she winced, dropping it on the floor.

"I've got it," she said, feeling stupid.

She groped for the lighter, then quickly walked to the front of the chapel, which was dotted with votive candles, a few burned down to the wick. A cigarette butt rested on the altar steps. She nudged it off with the toe of her boot.

"What are you doing on campus tonight, anyway?" she asked, trying to call attention away from her clumsiness as she carefully lit each votive. "Aren't you going back to New York for the holidays?"

If Thomas heard her, he didn't answer. The wicks of the candles popped and sizzled, illuminating a thick marble altar and the several rows of benches behind, probably meant for the choir.

"Thomas?" He was still at the back of the chapel, fiddling with a cell phone. After a few seconds, he snapped the phone closed and slipped it into Ariana's bag.

"What are you doing with my phone?" she demanded. How dare he go through her stuff?

"Letting Ryan know to not expect you."

He stuffed his hands in his pockets and headed down the aisle toward her.

Daniel. Goosebumps prickled her skin at the sound of Daniel's last name, and her throat was suddenly dry.

"What did you tell him?"

"Relax." Thomas laughed. "Told him you didn't finish your paper in time, and you couldn't get out of town tonight." He sat in front of the altar just a few steps below her and rubbed his hands quickly over his thighs. "So tonight, you're all mine, naughty girl."

Thomas sat down on a long wooden pew and pulled her down next to him, all in one swift motion. His blue eyes flashed in the candlelight, and warmth spread through Ariana's body like hot wax.

I love you, she thought. Then almost laughed at herself. How ridiculous—in love with Thomas Pearson. But she couldn't stop her heart from pounding. Couldn't stop her hands from grasping his jacket and pulling him to her. Didn't want to be anywhere but right here with him in this dark, cold place, even while the perfect boy waited for her at an exclusive resort with his wonderful family and some elaborate gift undoubtedly hidden away in his luggage.

What was that, if not love?

Thomas cupped her face in both hands and kissed her, this time with less urgency. It was sweet, soft, searching. As if he wanted to slowly take in every inch of her. Daniel had never kissed her like this. Never made her feel beautiful like this. He was more mechanical, stiff. This kiss was warm. It was right. It was . . . perfect.

Ariana relaxed into the moment, taking everything in. The hiss of the flickering candles, the snow falling on the dilapidated roof . . .

The sound of the chapel door, creaking open. Slamming shut.

They were not alone.

NEW

Panic hardened in Ariana's veins. She'd given in to herself for once in her life, done what felt right just one time, and she was about to get caught. What would her mother do when she found out Ariana had been expelled? She wasn't strong enough for this, for the humiliation that would come. Ariana was sure of that. Sure she'd be responsible for the aftermath. She jumped up and reached for her coat, which had somehow made its way off her shoulders once again.

"Don't stop on my account," a familiar voice called out.

Tentative relief spread through Ariana's body. Not a teacher. Not security. Thank God. She almost wanted to cry.

"Tate!" Thomas barked, jumping up. "You scared the shit out of us!"

Eli Tate, Thomas's former roommate, ambled down the aisle in dark jeans and a hoodie, a crooked grin plastered on his face. Even though Eli lived just a couple towns over in Connecticut, he hadn't been back to campus since his expulsion.

"Pearson!" Eli clasped hands with Thomas. "What's up, loser?" He laughed. "Miss me?" He nodded in Ariana's direction. "Hey."

Ariana tried to speak, but her throat felt constricted, dry. She nodded, wiping her sweaty palms on her wool pants.

"What the fuck are you doing here, man?" Thomas demanded, resting his forearms on his knees as Eli dropped down next to him on the bench.

"Better question is, what are *you* two doing here?" Eli flashed his familiar, impish grin.

"Just hanging out," Thomas said warily, catching Ariana's eye. "Ariana had to stay behind for a couple days to finish up some things."

"I bet," Eli snorted, letting his eyes linger on Ariana.

"So really, what are you doing here?" she asked quickly.

"Needed a break, so I trained in from Greenwich," he replied, stretching his arms over his head. "Evil stepsister number two is getting hitched next week, and if I had to sit around the house and hear one more screaming phone call to the florist, I was gonna lose it." He pulled something from his jacket pocket and rolled it between his fingers, examining it carefully. Ariana tried not to look obvious as she craned her neck a little to see what it was. A joint. "Thought I'd come over to campus and hang out. Didn't know you two were already staked out here." He smirked, giving his wiry curls a shake. He picked up one of the votives and held it to the end of the joint. He inhaled deeply, then paused. A sickeningly sweet smell hovered around him. "Shame they're tearing this place down."

"Yeah," Thomas said vaguely. "Shame."

Ariana thought she saw the beginnings of a smile in his eyes, but she wasn't sure. She had the sudden urge to tell Eli to leave. She'd gotten a taste of what being with Thomas was like, and she wanted more. Craved more. Her body still throbbed with anticipation, restless energy. She wanted Thomas alone. She needed to find out what could happen.

Eli passed the joint to Thomas. He closed his eyes and brought it to his lips. Ariana felt her body tensing. Would Thomas rather get high with Eli than spend time with her? He should have been thinking of ways to get Eli to leave. A spark of anger flared up inside of her.

Why did the men in her life always put her second? Her father, Daniel, Thomas. Why did she never come first?

"Ariana?" Thomas held the joint in her direction.

And just like that her irritation melted. He was still thinking of her, including her. Only she had never smoked before. It had never quite seemed *her*. But who the hell knew who she was, what she could do? Didn't just being here prove that?

"Why not?" she said casually, taking the joint from Thomas and praying she would do it right. She pinched the joint between her thumb and index finger and inhaled, just like Eli and Thomas had done. Her lungs burned, and she doubled over in a coughing fit. She could feel her cheeks burning in embarrassment, and tears sprang to her eyes.

Nice try, loser, a voice in her head taunted her. *Why do you even bother?*

"You okay?" Thomas asked gently, reaching out and touching her knee. Now that his touch was pitying, she didn't want it.

"M'fine," she choked out, jerking her knee away from him.

"Whoa." Eli laughed, propping himself up on his elbows. "Pearson's really starting to rub off on you. Last year when we were all in Cabo you wouldn't touch that shit. Remember? Gage did that prissy impression of her?" he asked, slapping Thomas on the shoulder.

Ariana's face burned. No one had ever told her that Gage had mocked her after that incident.

"I didn't go to Cabo last Christmas," Thomas reminded him. "My parents made me go to Switzerland. Blake was skiing in that big tournament thing."

"Riiiight. You missed one hell of a party, man," Eli said. "But then, so did Ariana," he said, nodding at her. "Girl refused to unclench the whole time."

"Well, a lot can change in a year," she snapped. *Although this one thing will stay the same.* She handed the joint back to Eli.

"Fair enough." Eli shrugged, taking another hit.

"So how long are you planning on sticking around, Tate?" Thomas asked, shooting Ariana a meaningful glance. Her heart skipped a beat.

Eli shrugged. "Depends on how long I can get away with ducking out on this wedding shit."

"It would probably mean a lot to your sister if you were there," Ariana said flatly. If she had to carry him back to Greenwich herself, she would.

"Stepsister," Eli corrected her. "And trust me, she doesn't care if I'm there or not, so long as she gets her fucking white silk tent in Aruba." He stood up, clapped Thomas on the back, and headed down the aisle for the door, the joint held tightly between his fingers.

"Are you leaving?" Ariana asked, aware that she sounded too hopeful.

"Gotta take a piss," he called over his shoulder.

Something seemed wrong about saying the word *piss* in a chapel. Then again, something seemed wrong about hooking up in a chapel with a guy who wasn't even her boyfriend. She wasn't in much of a position to judge.

"We've got to ditch him. ASAP," she whispered as the chapel doors slammed shut. She jumped to her feet, wrapping her coat tightly around her frame. "Get up." She extended her hand toward Thomas, the cold rushing over her again. Her fingers were tinged a light blue, her nose and ears completely numb.

Thomas looked up at her with a mixture of curiosity and amusement. "I think I like the new you."

She liked the new her too. Even in this frigid, abandoned space, with a boy she barely knew, she felt safe. Secure enough to say exactly what she wanted. She fiddled with the fleur-de-lis around her neck, wondering if this was what it felt like to be Noelle. To know what you wanted and expect to get it.

"Then let's go," she said playfully.

Thomas grinned and let her pull him to his feet. He glanced at the doors through which Eli had disappeared, then started in the opposite direction. "This way."

"Wait! My bag."

Ariana scurried over and grabbed up her things, then took Thomas's hand again. He tugged her toward an arched exit at the back of the church, and the rush of excitement that had stolen over her just minutes before seized her again. Outside, they stepped right into a drift of snow that came just below her knees. It seeped through her pants, melting against her skin, but she didn't care. She was warm all over.

Thomas led her into a small clearing behind the church, where the canopy of tree branches had prevented the snow from piling too deep. Wind swirled overhead and Eli was nowhere to be seen.

"So . . ." He grinned, barely visible in the dark. "You're the boss."

"We can't go back to Drake. Too many teachers around." Ariana tucked her hands into her coat pockets. "A hotel?" she mused. A sudden gust of wind sent a dusting of white powder into her face, and she turned to shield herself. "The Driscoll? It's close enough that we could walk, and it probably wouldn't take that long."

The thought of being with Thomas, alone, in a warm hotel room sent a shiver down her spine.

"Yeah." Thomas pulled his cell from his pocket and pressed a single button, holding the phone to his ear.

"Speed dial?" Ariana groaned. "I really wish I hadn't seen that."

"It's room service," Thomas said, trying to keep a straight face. Trying, but failing. "They make an unbelievable cheeseburger. Swear."

Ariana raised an eyebrow.

"You don't believe me?" Thomas pretended to be indignant.

"About as much as I believe you'd read *Playboy* for the articles."

Thomas held his hand up. "Yeah. Just wanted to book a room for tonight?" He paused, his face falling. "Okay. Thanks, man." He snapped the phone shut and shoved it back in his pocket. "They're booked. Guy at the desk said every hotel in town is packed. People can't get out of here because of the snow."

Ariana's heart sank. It was crazy to want to be alone in a hotel room with Thomas. Crazy to be here with him now. But she couldn't imagine being anywhere else.

"So I guess we only have one option," she said gravely. She nodded at the smooth covering of snow on the ground.

Thomas laughed, backing away from her. "Oh, no. No way. You're crazy."

It took every ounce of bravery Ariana could summon to do what she did next. She lowered her body to the freezing cold ground, leaned back on her elbows, and looked up at Thomas, her blue eyes tempting.

"Am I?"

She stopped breathing. She couldn't believe what she was saying. Doing.

Thomas's smile widened. "How could I say no to that?"

Ariana grinned, ecstatic and relieved all at once. He knelt down and buried his hands in her thick, blond hair before touching his lips to hers. Ariana's heart filled with pure happiness as he lowered himself on top of her. She didn't care about the cold anymore. Couldn't feel anything but the heat of his body. She turned her face to let him run his lips along her cheek and out of the corner of her eye, she saw a dark shape in the snow.

And froze.

"Thomas," she croaked, pushing him away. "Stop."

Bile rose in the back of her throat. She was seeing things. She must have been.

"What?" He squinted quizzically at her. "What's wrong?"

Her body felt as though it had been filled with lead, but her mind was racing. Screaming. *It wasn't possible. He couldn't have. . . .* She forced herself to sit up. Reached for the object and held it in front of Thomas, shaking the snow from it. She was going to throw up.

"What's that?" Thomas asked.

"Daniel's hat," she managed, fighting the nausea that swept over her. "He must have been here. He must have come back for me."

"No," Thomas said, looking around nonetheless. "He left this morning. This hat could belong to anyone. It could be Eli's or some other moron who was up here smoking."

But Ariana knew better. The hat was brand-new. Obviously unused. It was too much of a coincidence. Daniel had been here. He must have found out somehow and now he was watching her. He knew what she had done.

BREAKING AND ENTERING

"He knows." Ariana stared straight ahead, still clutching Daniel's hat. Numb to the icy chill that gripped her body and refused to release her. Numb to the snow that seemed to fall harder with each passing second. She felt nothing but fear. Every muscle in her body tensed, like those of a frightened, trapped animal.

"Ariana."

Hearing her name on his tongue made her want to cry. But she couldn't. The fear rose up in her throat, made it hard for her to breathe.

"Every guy on campus has a hat like that. It's like seeing a polo shirt in the snow and being positive it's Daniel's." He tugged the hat from her grip and chucked it into the woods. "Let's get out of here. It's freaking freezing."

Ariana nodded. "You're right." She let him pull her up and dusted the snow from her wet jeans. "That hat could be anybody's."

She was simply repeating the words Thomas wanted to hear. A small part of her knew she was being irrational, thinking Daniel was here, but he was the *worst* person to have seen them. The one person who could make everything fall apart at once. How could her mind not go there? Besides, she'd *just* given him that hat. What were the odds?

Another wave of panic gripped her as her mind raced over the events of the day. Daniel probably hadn't believed her lie about the text. What if he'd just pretended to believe it to save face in front of their friends, then stayed behind to make her pay? He didn't like to lose. That quality was what made him a star athlete. It made him a Ryan. The kind of guy who would do anything to keep from losing Ariana. *Anything.*

And if he was here somewhere, following her and Thomas, there was no telling what he'd do.

"Come on. We can stay in Ketlar." Thomas grabbed her hand, but her fingers were too cold to feel him.

"Ketlar's not open."

She clung to him as if he could erase the fear. Make it not true. Make that hat somehow not be there.

"I rigged the back door. We can stay in my room." He stepped ahead of her as they reached the edge of the woods, leaning against a thick, snow-covered pine branch so Ariana could pass through.

"I don't know," Ariana said, pausing as the wind whipped her hair around her face. "What if someone sees us? We can't get caught. And what if Daniel—"

"Daniel's not here!" Thomas shouted against the wind, releasing her hand. His tone was sharp, stinging, and Ariana took a shocked step back.

"I'm sorry," she muttered, not knowing exactly what she was apologizing for.

Thomas's shoulders dropped. "No. I mean, *I'm* sorry." His voice softened and he looked off to the right, toward the school. Away from her. "It's just, I'm sick of hearing about Daniel Ryan."

Ariana's heart warmed at the vulnerability in this statement.

"And I'm aware that we can't get caught. I'm screwed if I get expelled," he said. "But I can't think of any other options."

"Fine," Ariana said. "We'll go to Ketlar."

He reached for her hand again and they walked the rest of the way in silence. As she trudged through the snow, bent against the wind, Ariana tried to get her feelings in order. Thomas's tone had wounded her. It had made her feel like a scolded child. Plus, why did he care so much about getting caught? He always got away with everything. And he wasn't the one who had everything to lose if he got expelled. He wasn't the one whose family would be destroyed if he was caught. When they reached the back door of Ketlar, Thomas easily pulled it open.

"The wonders of duct tape," he said, pointing to the metallic strip he'd secured over the lock. He pulled his lighter from his pocket and ignited it, then gestured for Ariana to go in ahead of him.

The halls were eerily lifeless. Usually filled with laughter and loud music, they now echoed with heavy silence. Ariana shivered in the cold, watching her breath rise and disappear in front of her. Silently, she followed him to the second floor, turning away as they passed Daniel's room.

They stopped at the end of the hall, in front of Thomas's door. It was bare, unlike most of the other doors on the hall, which were covered in bumper stickers, dry-erase boards, and pictures. He pushed the door open with his free hand.

"It's not exactly a room at the Driscoll," he announced, holding the lighter in front of them. "But it should work. At least for tonight."

The security lights on the quad afforded enough light for Ariana to see the state of Thomas's room. It looked almost identical to the space she shared with Noelle, except it was about half the size. Thomas's side of the room was sparse and neat. His thin plaid bed-spread was stretched tightly over his single bed, and the desk next to it was almost bare, with the exception of a few sharpened pencils in a pencil holder and an empty fifth of Captain Morgan's. The essentials. The other side of the room was littered with dirty clothes and textbooks. A large metal sign that said, IT'S MILLER TIME, hung over a cluttered desk, and the bed was unmade.

"Classy," she said wryly. "Did you rob a liquor store?"

"Harsh words from someone who just committed a felony." Thomas smirked. "Breaking and entering. Considering your reputa-tion, I would have expected more from you."

Ariana exhaled slowly. It seemed that the tension between them had dissolved as quickly as it had appeared. And knowing that they were together in Thomas's room, out of the storm—out of sight—made her feel safe. She dropped her bag on Thomas's desk chair.

"You seem to be forgetting that I'm not the one breaking and entering here. I'm just the accomplice."

"Nice try. But you're in this just as deep as I am. If I go down, you're coming with me." For a moment, the shadows moving across Thomas's face made him look different. Like a stranger. Dangerous. But then he smiled and he was Thomas again. "Let me get the light."

"Don't." Ariana said quickly, reaching for him. She gripped his sleeve. "Someone might notice." She didn't want to tell him that there was something in her that needed to keep the relative darkness between them. Knowing that he couldn't entirely see her face, couldn't read her, would make it easier for her to get closer to him.

"Good call, naughty girl."

He let the lighter go dark and leaned toward her. All the tiny hairs on Ariana's neck stood on end and her lips pursed, anticipating his kiss. But then he leaned right past her and opened his top desk drawer, plucking out a pair of candles.

"Interesting," she said, raising an eyebrow and sliding aside to give him more room. "This wouldn't be some sort of ploy to seduce me, would it?"

Thomas placed the candles on his desk and quickly lit them, then glanced at her over his shoulder. "Like I really need candles."

Ariana blushed as her heart flipped over ten times. How did anyone get so confident? It was intoxicating. Thomas turned and dropped down on his bed, looking up at her with a cocky smile in the flickering light.

"You gonna stand there all night?" he asked slyly. "Much warmer over here."

Ariana didn't move. Suddenly, now that she was here—now that she was faced with the stark reality of being alone with Thomas, being in bed with him—she couldn't do it. What was she thinking? That she was going to lose her virginity to him right here, right now? After telling Daniel that she couldn't sleep with him in a dorm room? After putting off her perfect boyfriend for so long, was she really going to give it up to Thomas Pearson?

Besides, Daniel might have followed them here. He might be standing outside the door right now, listening. The very thought sent the walls closing in on her. There was no telling what he would do if he heard the wrong thing.

"I can't," she said.

Thomas's smile froze. "You're kidding."

"I'll just sleep in your roommate's bed," Ariana told him, trying not to cringe as she sat at the very edge of the other bed. The faint smell of spoiled milk leaked from a mini fridge under her bed.

"Wait a second. First you have me calling the Driscoll Hotel and now you're all shy?" Thomas challenged, propping himself up on one elbow to see her.

"Don't be mad," Ariana said.

"I'm not mad. Just curious," he replied. "Split personalities interest me."

"I'm not crazy," Ariana snapped.

Thomas stared at her for a long moment. So long that Ariana almost started to squirm.

"Fine. Whatever you want." Thomas shrugged.

He got up and stripped down to his boxers right in front of her. Then he got right into bed, tunneling under the covers.

"But you should know that my roommate's kind of a man whore. I've seen some pretty skanky girls coming in and out of this room. And I gotta tell you, in the four months I've known the guy, I've never seen him wash his sheets. No telling what kind of—"

"I'll sleep on top of the sheets," Ariana said. She glanced around her for a comforter. There wasn't one. She could already feel the sharp cold settling into her bones. She shivered, pressing her face into the sheets to warm her nose. They smelled like mildew. She glanced over at Thomas. If he was a gentleman, he would offer her a blanket. Or at least some sweats or something. Anything dry and warm.

"Nice and warm over here," Thomas said with an exaggerated yawn. "Biohazard-free, too."

Her fists clenched in indignation. "How nice for you."

She was not going to ask him for clothes. She refused. Instead, she pulled off her sweater to get the wet sleeves away from her skin, exposing the white T-shirt underneath. Then she yanked her coat over her body, trying to keep the wet outside layer away from her. She pulled her knees to her chest and wrapped her arms around them, curling into a tight ball. She was colder than ever.

"Yup. Nice and warm," Thomas sang, cuddling further under his blankets. "Toasty, really. Toasty, toasty, toasty . . ."

"For God's sake," she snapped, sitting up. "If I come over there, will you shut up and go to sleep?"

He lifted up the covers and slid back toward the wall, giving her room. "Neither one of us is going to get any sleep."

Ariana was glad Thomas couldn't see the flush that crept from neck into her face.

"We'll see," she said.

She dropped down next to him and turned over so her back was to him. As he settled the blankets over her body he let his arm drape around her waist. Despite her early protestations, she luxuriated in the warmth.

"Now what?" Thomas whispered in her ear, sending pleasant shivers all down her side.

"Now we sleep," she told him firmly, even though her entire body was tingling.

"Sure," he said. "You just wake me when you can't take it anymore."

Ariana said nothing, but she lay there, awake, as Thomas slowly fell asleep, worried that if she moved even slightly he might think she was coming on to him. Worried that at any second Daniel would open the lockless door and catch them together. But after watching the digital clock tick from minute to minute for over an hour, after listening for footfalls in the hallway that never came, she finally let the sound of Thomas's steady breathing lull her to sleep.

THE MORNING AFTER

Ariana jolted upright, her chest heaving. Ragged, uneven gasps filled the air around her. The familiar nightmare, cut together like a terrifying collage, had woken her. The empty bottle of wine, the trace of her own screams, the blinding flash of fluorescent light. And her mother's voice.

You never know what people are capable of until they're pushed to their edge.

She shivered and looked around for something familiar. But there was no picture of her on the desk. No Christmas lights around the windows. No neat stacks of worn novels piled next to her bed. Just a soccer ball wedged under the desk and a near-empty bottle of Captain Morgan.

Her breathing slowed as she realized where she was. Releasing Thomas's plaid bedspread from her grip, she glanced down at him. He slept on his stomach, his head turned toward her. She watched his body rise and fall calmly next to her. His mouth was slightly parted, his breathing even. She tried to ignore the twinge of jealousy she felt. She hadn't slept like that in too long. Not since the nightmares had started, just over a year ago.

She turned to find her sweater and a hand on her back made her jump. She reminded herself that it was just Thomas. Just Thomas.

"You seem tense, naughty girl," Thomas yawned behind her. "Luckily, I happen to know a few ways to calm you down," he added suggestively, pulling her back down. He wrapped his warm arms around her from behind and cuddled into her back, their bodies melding together.

Ariana forced a laugh, not turning around. "I should go," she said softly, without moving. She knew she should pull away from him. Should get up and walk out the door. Go to Vermont. End this thing with Thomas, whatever it was, while she still could. But the strength of his arms seemed to soothe her. They were so close she could feel his heart beating. Her whole body slowed under his touch, making it impossible for her to do the right thing.

"You're not getting out of here any time soon. Not if I have anything to do with it."

She wanted to tell him that he didn't have anything to do with it, didn't have any say in what she did. But she would have been lying. And she couldn't bear the thought of being both a cheat and a liar. That wasn't her. It couldn't be her. She wouldn't be able to live with herself.

"Did you sleep okay?" she asked.

"Sure." Thomas softly brushed her hair aside and kissed the back of her neck. His words hummed on her clammy skin. "But I would have preferred that neither of us got any sleep." He slid his hands across her hips and started to move them up her stomach.

She raised her hands to his, stopping him, and rolled over to face him. He had a crease on one side of his face, stubble covered his chin and cheeks, and his hair stuck up in back. But even with all this, he was still so handsome.

"Tell me something about you," she said.

She needed to hear something that would justify all this. Something that would make it okay that she was here with him instead of on the slopes with Daniel. She needed him to make this okay.

Thomas smirked, bringing his lips close to her ear. "Why?" he whispered.

Chills shot down her spine, and suddenly it didn't matter if he made it okay. All she wanted to do was kiss him. "Because." Ariana was so breathless as she looked up at him, she could hardly form the words. "Because we just spent the night in the same bed and we hardly know each other."

As she looked into his eyes, she realized that wasn't really true. They might not have spent much time together, might not have known the small details, but somehow, she knew him. He knew her. She could feel it in the way her mind, her body responded whenever he looked at her. Even if she didn't know his middle name or whether he'd worn braces or if he loved his parents . . . she *knew* him.

"Well, I've never actually told anyone this," Thomas said softly, his face serious. "But I'm psychic."

"Psychic?" she repeated.

"Yeah," he said earnestly. He was so close now his nose was touching hers. The light contact sent her blood racing. "Like for example, I know that in five seconds, you're going to kiss me."

Ariana's heart slammed into her rib cage over and over. "Oh, yeah?" she said playfully.

"Yeah."

Daniel would *kill* her if he knew what she was doing right now— what she was thinking. But she didn't care. At that moment it didn't matter. All she wanted was to be with Thomas. To let herself go. To let him do whatever he wanted.

"Four . . ." Thomas flashed his perfect, boyish grin.

"Not gonna happen," Ariana joked.

"Three . . ."

"You're going to have to kiss me first."

"Two . . ."

He shut his eyes.

"Uh-uh . . ." she sang.

"One."

Ariana closed her eyes and waited for the kiss she knew was coming. Then her cell phone rang. Automatically, her head shot up and she knocked skulls with Thomas. Hard.

"Sonofa—"

Thomas released her and fell back, hand to his forehead.

"Sorry! I'm sorry," Ariana said, ignoring the pain as she groped for her phone in her bag. When she finally found it, the display said that she had a new text message. Heart pounding, she quickly opened it.

Daniel: Can't get warm up here without u. Call and let me know ur ok.

Ariana was crushed by a sudden wave of nausea.

"Who's that?" Thomas asked, his face still contorted with pain.

"Nothing," Ariana said quickly. "No one."

She slung her legs over the side of the bed and got up to crack the window. Snow swirled outside, blanketing the entire campus with a fresh coating of white. There were at least two feet of thick powder. Ariana had never seen so much snow in her life, and she let the cold air pour over her and wash the nausea away. She felt as if she'd just been caught in the act. That Daniel had somehow known the exact moment to text her to keep her from doing what she was about to do with Thomas.

Flipping open her phone, she read the text again.

Okay. Just breathe. Breathe and think this through.

In . . . two . . . three . . .

Out . . . two . . . three . . .

And suddenly, her mind cleared. Daniel was waiting for her in Vermont. This meant that the hat in the woods really *was* a coincidence. He wasn't still on campus. He didn't know what she had been doing. Which meant that she could still fix this. She could still turn back and make this all okay.

Ariana took in another breath of icy morning air and held it, staring out at the gray early morning light. She had never seen campus from this angle before. She'd been in Ketlar plenty of times, but always on the other side of the building, where Daniel's sloppy disaster of a room was located. She thought of all those nights he'd helped her sneak past Mr. Cross, the Ketlar Hall advisor. How he always let her wear his favorite, worn Harvard sweatshirt when she got cold. How warm and cozy she always felt when they cuddled while watching movies on his laptop. How he always walked her back to Billings no matter what time it was, risking getting caught every time.

Maybe it wasn't exhilarating and dangerous like the last fourteen hours with Thomas had been, but it was her life. The life she was supposed to have. The life her mother wanted for her. Thomas Pearson could not be part of that life.

"Something wrong, naughty girl?" Thomas asked, walking to the window and snaking his arms around her from behind.

Cold, dark rage instantly overcame her. The arms that had made her feel so safe moments ago suddenly burned her skin.

"Let go of me," she snapped, ripping herself away from him.

Thomas took a step back, startled, but Ariana barely noticed. Her mind was racing off on a horrible tangent and she couldn't stop it. She was dirt. She was nothing. She wasn't worthy of Daniel Ryan. Look what she'd done to him. Look where she was while he was waiting for her in Vermont. Look who she was *with*. Ariana grabbed her sweater off the extra bed and clutched it in both hands, twisting it into a spiral. Daniel would die if he knew.

Guilt crashed down on her in merciless waves. Each time she tried to catch her breath, another swept over her, dragging her under. She doubled over, gasping for air, fighting the bile that surged from her stomach to the back of her throat. Tears stung her eyes.

"Ariana, what's wrong?" Thomas reached out and rested his hand on her back.

She jerked away. "Don't touch me!"

"Sorry." A surprised look passed over Thomas's face, and he held his hands up in surrender.

"I have to go. I have to shower."

She felt so dirty. So awful she could hardly stand to be in her own skin.

"Okay. Okay, fine. I'll come with you and show you where the—"

"No!" Ariana whirled on him. What did he think they were going to do, shower *together*? She couldn't believe he was still coming on to her. Couldn't this guy take a hint? "I'm not showering with you. I have to get out of here. I have to get away from you."

Ariana sat and yanked her boots on, angry tears spilling down her cheeks.

"Okay. What the hell just happened here?" Thomas demanded.

Ariana looked up at him. He was still shirtless. Standing there in his boxers. Disgusted, Ariana looked away and shoved her hair behind her shoulders.

"What just happened is, I woke up. I realized what I'm doing, how *wrong* this is," she spat. "I'm going to Vermont. I'm going to be with Daniel. This was a mistake."

Thomas's face was saturated with confusion. Ariana felt a new wave of guilt, but she couldn't let him get to her. He was not important. Not anymore. She had to focus.

Daniel . . . Daniel is the one I need.

"Fine." In an instant, Thomas's face hardened and he took a step back toward the bed. "Good luck getting out of here in this weather. And try not to get caught. If I'm gonna get a third strike, it's not gonna be for you."

"What?" Ariana blurted. She stood and snatched up her coat and bag.

"You're not the only one who has something to lose here," Thomas yelled, yanking a long-sleeved T-shirt on over his head. "I'm not gonna get expelled just because Easton's resident prude wanted to use me for the lamest walk on the wild side ever."

Without even thinking, Ariana slapped Thomas clean across the face. Then, while he was still standing there, stunned, she turned and stormed out of his room, slamming the door behind her. Her palm stung from the contact as she hurried down the hallway and into the stairwell, fumbling with her phone. Daniel's cell went right to voice mail. Ariana took a deep breath and concentrated on sounding chipper.

"Daniel, hi. I'm so sorry. I got caught in this stupid storm, but I'm doing everything I can to get there. I'll see you soon." She took the stairs two at a time, but she wasn't breathing. If she breathed he would hear that she was upset. "I love you," she added quickly.

Then she burst out into the cold, gasping for air. Wind whipped past her, nearly knocking her off her feet as icy snow pelted her face. But the frigid air cleared away everything else and Ariana started to feel in control again. It was okay. It was all going to be okay.

Her moment of insanity was over.

NOT SORRY

Lukewarm water spilled from the showerhead over Ariana's smooth, pale skin. She'd been so desperate to get away from Thomas that she had almost used her electronic key to enter Billings through the front door, then remembered at the last second that she wasn't supposed to be on campus, and that security would be alerted if someone tried to enter any dorm other than Drake. Cursing herself for nearly messing up so badly, she had trudged around to the back and used Mrs. Lattimer's key to get in through the rear door. Noelle had had the key made at the beginning of the semester, in anticipation of the many times she wouldn't make it back to Billings in time for curfew. She kept it wedged behind one of the wrought iron sconces that illuminated the back entrance. Ariana was the only other person on campus who knew about the key, but she'd never had to use it. Until now.

Exhausted, she leaned against the frosted glass shower door. The large sea foam green bathroom tiles were usually calming, usually made the shower feel like a spa—her own small oasis. But today they just seemed hard and cold. She flinched as the water temperature dipped, then rose again. She knew that it didn't matter how long she stood under the water. The guilt would be impossible to rinse away.

She had to believe that it wasn't too late to fix things. If she could just get to Vermont, everything would be fine. She would remember that she loved Daniel, and why. Remember all the sweet things he had done for her in their year together.

And there had been so many. As she worked her coconut-scented shampoo through her tangled hair, she smiled at the memory of her birthday last spring. Daniel had shown up at her door in jeans and a T-shirt, holding a bottle of Clos du Mesnil. They'd taken a car to Manhattan, where he'd surprised her with a private literary tour of the West Village. They roamed the quaint streets together, exploring her favorite American authors' haunts. Shared a bottle of red wine in a tiny, poorly lit bar overlooking Washington Square, where Henry James was said to have struggled through *The Wings of the Dove*. Downed a tall mug of dark beer at Chumley's, where she could almost feel the ghosts of Fitzgerald and Hemingway in the next booth over. For an entire afternoon, she'd been transported to a place where she didn't have to worry about her family, or making good grades, or keeping Paige Ryan happy so she would get a bid at Billings. She could lose herself in another time, in the stories she loved so much. And Daniel had done it all for her. Because he loved her.

He showed it every day, in the way he was so protective of her. Like that thing with Sergei the other night. Like . . .

Suddenly the memory of that awful night back in August came rushing back to Ariana and her eyes popped open. She didn't want to remember what Daniel had done that night, but the images came back in full color nonetheless. All the Billings Girls and their boyfriends had been hanging out in the woods, a last gathering before classes started. Ariana was snuggled against Daniel in front of the fire, sipping a beer, when she felt his body tense beside her. He'd accused one of Dash's buddies from home of staring at Ariana, and just like that, Daniel had snapped.

Ariana squeezed her eyes closed again and braced her hand against the wall, trying to block it out, but she couldn't. She heard the crack as the guy was slammed back against a tree. The sick, dull thud of Daniel's fists as they hit him again and again. The pathetic pleading, over and over and over again.

Please, man . . . I didn't mean anything . . . please stop. . . .

Finally, Dash had dragged Daniel off and helped his friend back to his car, but everyone else had acted as if nothing out of the ordinary had happened. Paige had shrugged it off with a roll of her eyes and a "That's my brother." Even Noelle had seemed impressed that Daniel would go so far to protect his territory.

His territory. Me, Ariana thought.

Her skin prickled with heat even as the water turned colder. She had to get out of the shower before she got pneumonia. As she grasped the shower nozzle and turned it all the way to the left, the sound of screeching pipes echoed in the bathroom, but the water temperature didn't change. Ariana held her breath and ducked under the chilly spray, combing the shampoo out of her hair with her fingers.

Something caught her ear and Ariana froze. Had she just heard a creak, or was she imagining things? Out of the corner of her eye, she saw a shadow slip by. She grabbed her arm, anxiously digging her fingernails into her flesh.

"Hello? Thomas? Is that you?"

Nothing. But she was sure someone was there. Who was it? Was some random person watching her? For a long moment, Ariana didn't move. She simply held her breath and listened. There was nothing. It was her imagination. She was seeing things.

Then, another creak. Ariana turned off the icy cold water.

"Hello?" she called. The word hovered in the air a moment after she'd spoken. "Is someone there?"

Silence.

She opened the shower door a crack. The bathroom was empty. Single drops of water were falling slowly from the porcelain sink. But it had been dripping earlier, too, right? And everything was in its place: Noelle's cubby stocked with shampoo, loofahs, and expensive clay facial masques; Ariana's electric toothbrush; her towel, draped over the bench just outside the shower door. She blinked. Strange. She could have sworn she'd hung it on the door hook. She *always* hung it on the hook.

She shook her head. It was just her imagination. That was all. She was in Billings, alone, for the first time, and it was creeping her out. She'd obviously been rushed and upset and put her clothes in a different place. Not a big deal. She exhaled a shaky sigh of relief and reached for her towel.

Suddenly, the door to the bathroom swung open. Ariana screamed.

"Perfect timing," Thomas Pearson said with a leer.

"Thomas!" Ariana screeched, wrapping the towel around her as tightly as possible. "You scared the shit out of me!"

Oh my God, Thomas Pearson just saw me naked. Completely. Naked.

His features contorted, like he was trying to keep a straight face. There was snow in his hair and his cheeks had turned adorably pink from the cold. "Sorry. I mean, sorry I scared you. Not that I saw you naked. Just to be clear."

"That's not funny." She closed the door again, putting the foggy glass between the two of them, and huddled in the corner to take a breath, hand to her chest. "What are you doing here?"

Thomas walked into the bathroom. She could hear him rifling through the medicine cabinet over the sink. "Just wanted to give you a chance to apologize. You know, for being such a bitch."

Ariana froze as she toweled off her hair. There was a casual tone in his voice. He was joking. Now that she'd had a chance to cool off, she felt the humiliation of her overreaction back in his room, and decided to follow his lead. Pretend it was no big deal.

"Why didn't you answer when I said your name?" she asked.

There was a pause. "What do you mean? I just got here."

"But I just heard you a few minutes ago," she protested. "You were in the bathroom." She secured the towel around her and opened the door. Thomas looked genuinely confused. Ariana's heart thumped with fear. "You really just got here?"

"Swear."

But someone had been there. She was sure of it. Was Thomas lying?

Or was Daniel on campus messing with her? Or had it been someone else entirely? Ariana's empty stomach turned dangerously.

"How did you get in?" she demanded.

"Noelle's key," he replied simply, perusing the bath products next to the shower. He picked up a giant jar of conditioner, inspecting the label. "What the hell is jojoba oil?"

"How do you know about Noelle's key?" She stepped onto the woven bath mat and hugged herself against the cool air.

"Common knowledge, naughty girl."

Common knowledge. Noelle had probably told Dash about it. Which meant that Paige probably knew about it, too. And Daniel.

Thomas put the jar down and took an uncertain step toward her.

"Give me a second." She held the door to her room open. "I'll be right out."

"I'll be right here," Thomas said with a suggestive smile before closing the door behind him.

Alone again, Ariana leaned against the wall and tried to slow her breathing. What if Daniel *was* here? What if he was inside Billings right now, listening in on her and Thomas?

But no. No. It couldn't be. He wouldn't skip out on his parents, his sister, their Christmas vacation, just to mess with her. He wouldn't. She had to believe that. She had to believe it or she was going to go insane.

"Just deal with the current problem," she whispered, wiping the fog off the mirror and staring at her reflection.

Thomas.

What was she going to do? She had thought this was over. Thought that slap, for better or for worse, had put a stop to this insanity. But now, here Thomas was, in her room. They were alone and her skin was humming again. She took a deep breath and slipped into her white silk robe.

She had to tell him they couldn't do this anymore. Maybe it was intriguing and fun, but it couldn't be real. What she had with Daniel was real. Yes. That was what she was going to tell him, and he would just have to understand. She looked into the mirror, into her own blue eyes, and steeled herself for the conversation. But when she reached for the door handle a minute later, she realized she was still shaking. And it wasn't from the cold.

PLEADING MANTRA

"Thomas, I—"

Ariana's words died on her tongue as Thomas held out a pair of Noelle's sexiest underwear—a red thong with a tiny wedge of fabric at the front.

"Are these yours or Noelle's? 'Cuz I gotta say, my imagination is going to some pretty sweet places right now. . . ."

"They're not mine," she said, snatching them away from him and tossing them onto Noelle's bed with all the other clothes that hadn't made the cut for her trip home. "Thomas, listen—"

"Look, I just came over here to make peace because it looks like we're going to be stuck here for a couple of days," Thomas said, pushing his hands into the front pockets of his jeans. "And I still haven't heard that apology for teeing off on me."

Ariana clutched her arm again. "What do you mean, stuck here?"

Thomas gestured at Ariana's computer, which was showing

streaming video of a weather forecast. Clearly he'd helped himself to her Internet connection. She reached over and turned up the
volume.

". . . highway has been closed and all mass transit is suspended
for the duration of the storm," the weatherman was saying as he
was assaulted by wind and snow. "The governor has declared a state
of emergency and all nonessential personnel have been told to stay
home. The fewer people on the roads, the better. . . ."

Ariana's heart felt sick as she turned the volume down again.

"It's a nightmare out there," Thomas said.

Ariana turned and stared out the window. All she could see was
white. It was like an opaque veil had been wrapped tightly around
Billings House, trapping her inside.

"We're stuck," she said slowly, her mouth dry. "Together."

"Yeah, but don't worry. I won't do anything to make you smack me
again," Thomas said, his blue eyes dancing.

"You won't?" Ariana asked dumbly. She felt like she was just
waking up. Just realizing that Vermont was not going to happen. It was
taking her brain a minute to adjust.

"I'm not an idiot. I get the point. You're not going to cheat on
Daniel," Thomas said. "So if you want, we can be stuck here as
friends."

He looked her directly in eye. No fidgeting, no innuendo, no cocky
grin.

"Just friends," she said cautiously.

She wasn't sure if she could be friends with Thomas Pearson. Or that she wanted to be. But she did know that she didn't want to be stuck in this room alone. She couldn't do that. Not without losing her mind.

"Just friends," Thomas said.

"Fine."

Ariana nodded and started rooting through her dresser for warm clothes. Just friends was good. She could do this. If she just concentrated on Daniel, she could ignore Thomas's eyes. His smile. The memory of his bare chest pressed against her back all night. She could. Really.

"Cool. So, as my friend, I have this story that I *have* to tell you." Thomas plopped down on her bed. The bedsprings creaked loudly. "I just walked in on this smoking hot girl in the shower, and she was totally nak—"

Ariana clamped her hand over his mouth. Thomas looked up at her like she was nuts, but she kept her gaze trained on her door. She'd heard something. In the hallway. And this time, she definitely hadn't imagined it.

Thomas grabbed her wrist and pulled her hand away from his mouth. "What?" he said, following her gaze.

"Someone's here," she whispered.

Thomas scoffed. "There's nobody here but—" He stopped at the clear sound of footsteps nearing the door. "Shit!"

He jumped up and she practically shoved him into Noelle's walk-in closet. They ducked inside and closed the door quietly behind them. Ariana stepped directly onto a stiletto heel with her bare foot and had to bite her lip to keep from crying out. She cursed herself for choosing Noelle's closet. It might have been bigger than hers, but it was crammed with so many clothes, shoes, and bags that she and Thomas barely fit inside. Their bodies were pressed against each other, and she could feel Thomas's warm breath on her shoulder. Suddenly, she was aware of the fact that there was nothing but her thin robe between the two of them. Her skin pulsed with fear and excitement.

Then the door to her room slowly creaked open and Ariana forgot everything but her fear. She held her breath, leaning against Thomas for support, her skin slick with sweat. Someone crept into her room and across the creaky wood floor. A desk drawer slammed and Ariana gripped Thomas tighter. Whoever was out there was rifling through her things. Rage bubbled up inside of her, but she swallowed the urge to open the closet door.

Let it go. Just let it go. . . .

She *had* to let it go. She couldn't risk getting caught on campus. Headmaster Cox had been very clear about his rules.

A deep rumbling rose from Ariana's stomach, and she cringed and wrapped her arms tightly around her waist in a weak attempt to muffle the noise. She felt Thomas's body shaking with silent laughter. Until now, she hadn't even thought about the fact that she hadn't eaten since the day before.

The footsteps got closer to the closet and stopped in front of it. She screwed her eyes shut.

Please, Please just leave. Go. Go. Go.

Ariana gripped her arm in desperation. She pictured her mother, getting the news that her only daughter had been expelled from Easton. Pictured her alone, in that big, empty house. Flipping through photo albums filled with the pictures Ariana had sent almost every month since she'd arrived at Easton. Pictures of her and Daniel. Of dances and picnics and Daniel's lacrosse games. Of her and Noelle hanging out in their room. Of the dark, regal buildings that cast foreboding shadows over campus.

If Ariana was expelled, if Easton was gone and Billings was no longer a part of Ariana's life, her mother would have nothing to be proud of anymore. Without those places, those things, those people, Ariana was nothing. Nobody. And her mother would have nothing to live for. Ariana trembled with terror at the thought.

Finally, the footsteps moved away from the closet, and a few seconds later, the door to Ariana's room slammed shut. Instantly, Ariana burst out of the closet. She was dying to go for the door and catch the intruder in the hallway, but she knew she couldn't.

"Ariana, you're shaking," Thomas said, reaching for her.

"I know I'm shaking! There was someone in my room!" she hissed in response. She dove at her desk and started checking her desk drawers. She was torn between relief and rage. No one was supposed to be in Billings. Just how many people knew about Noelle's key? Besides, what would anybody want in her room? "Who the hell *was* that?"

"A teacher, maybe? Checking all the rooms to make sure everybody's out?" Thomas sounded uncertain.

She shook her head. "A teacher wouldn't go through my stuff. And they're all supposed to be in Drake, anyway."

She paused in front of her desk, letting her gaze wander from her laptop to her copy of *Madame Bovary*, and over the candle Daniel had brought her a few days before. Something didn't seem right. Something was missing.

Thomas shrugged. "Who knows? As long as we don't get caught, we're okay."

"How can you be so casual about this?" she snapped, running her hands over the surface of her desk. The thought that someone had been here, had been going through her things, made her skin crawl. "Someone was—" A splinter slipped underneath the surface of her skin. "Shit." She winced, peering down at the drop of blood that appeared on her fingertip. "Someone was going through my personal things, and you're acting like it was no big deal."

"It's just . . . there's nothing you can do about it, so there's no reason to get all stressed out." Thomas walked over to window, his shoulder lightly brushing her. She felt him pull away quickly, as if he had just burned himself. "It's not like you can go to the headmaster. We're not even supposed to be here."

Ariana ignored him, focusing for a moment on the splinter wedged in the tip of her throbbing finger. Why couldn't she figure out what was wrong, what was different with her desk? Something had changed. Just like something had changed in the bathroom between the time she'd gotten in the shower and the moment Thomas had appeared.

"Can we forget about this?" Thomas sighed. "Put on some clothes and let's get you something to eat before your stomach rats us out to the entire campus."

"Fine. I just need to figure out what's missing from my—"

Ariana's throat closed as her blood ran cold. She had just realized what was different. Whoever had been in her room had passed up her laptop, her diamond earrings, her delicate antique watch, and had taken only one thing.

The black-and-white picture of Ariana—the one Daniel had taken of her in the Hamptons—was gone.

PANCAKES AND GRILLED CHEESE

Daniel. It had to be. Who else would have broken into her room and taken only a picture of her? A picture *Daniel* had taken. Who else?

Ariana felt suddenly exhausted as she quickly threw on a pair of fresh jeans and a blue cashmere sweater. Thomas was waiting for her in the hallway, but she had to take a moment to just think.

If it was Daniel, why was he torturing her like this? Why not just come out and confront her? He was hotheaded, quick to anger. The way he'd jumped Dash's friend . . . But maybe he'd been so hurt by what she'd done, he'd decided to torture her, *then* confront her. The possibilities, the not knowing, were making her head hurt.

"How long does it take to put on a sweater?" Thomas asked, barging into the room. He blinked as she looked up, her shoulders slumped forward. "Oh. You're dressed."

"Didn't you tell me to get dressed?" she asked flatly.

"Yeah, but I thought if I surprised you I might catch the second act of *Nothing but Skin*," he joked.

Ariana leveled him with a no-nonsense stare. "I thought we were going to be just friends."

"We are." Thomas rolled his eyes. "Now let's go. I'm starving."

Ariana hesitated. "Thomas . . . you don't think it was Daniel who was in here before, do you?"

Thomas stopped on his way to the door. He tipped his head back and sighed at the ceiling. When he turned to her again, his expression was almost condescending, like he was about to explain some simple math concept to a first-grader.

"Ariana. Your boy's not here. He's in Vermont. The hat we saw was one of a million just like it around here. A coincidence. And yeah, somebody came in here. But it was probably just the housekeeper." Something in his eyes told Ariana he wasn't as confident about the intruder explanation as he was about the others. "Either way, we've gotta eat, right?"

"Right," she sighed. The heat had been turned off in the dorm and she was still cold, so she pulled her coat on over her clothes.

"So come on. I've got a surprise for you."

He turned and started rummaging through her desk drawers.

"What are you doing?" Ariana demanded, annoyed. Why did people keep touching her stuff?

He held up a silver paper clip. "Just call me Pearson," he said smoothly. "Thomas Pearson."

"What—"

Thomas held a finger to his perfect lips. Then he swiped Noelle's favorite Donna Karan tank top from her bed and sauntered toward Ariana, swinging the practically nonexistent piece of fabric in his hand. In a single move, he wrapped it tightly around her head, like a makeshift blindfold.

"Thomas, I'm really not in the mood for this."

She lifted her hands toward the blindfold, but Thomas gently grabbed them away, holding them both down in front of her as he faced her.

"Exactly. If we're stuck together until the weather lets up, I'm gonna need you to snap out of this mood. You're bringing me down, Osgood." His tone was light, but Ariana heard something strained in his voice.

"Fine," she reluctantly agreed.

"Good." He slipped behind her and clamped his hands on her shoulders, coaxing her slowly across the room. "Door," he announced, steering her carefully into the hallway.

Ariana opened her eyes and tried to make out shapes through the flimsy fabric. Everything was muddled and distorted. Her heart started to pound. She didn't like this one bit. Didn't like the total lack of control.

"I don't know why I have to be the one who's blindfolded," Ariana said in a clipped tone.

"Because I'm the one who knows where we're going, Einstein."

As he guided her through the dark hallway, he softly hummed the James Bond theme song in Ariana's ear. The reverberations of his voice sent pleasant shivers down her neck and over her shoulders, and somehow, she started to relax. She was in good hands. Thomas's hands.

"Stairs!" he sang.

Ariana smiled in spite of herself. Together they started down the stairs, Thomas's grip on her shoulders tightening to keep her from falling if she missed a step. But Ariana was nothing if not meticulous. She noted exactly how her feet were supposed to fall to keep her on track, making sure she stepped exactly the right distance each time.

"Here we are." Ariana heard him fumbling with a lock, then heard the slow creak of an opening door. He rested his hand on the small of her back. "Go ahead."

The whole blindfold game had been totally pointless. Billings was a small house, and Ariana knew exactly where they were.

"Thomas. You didn't," she said, yanking the tank top from over her eyes.

"What?" Thomas asked, smiling triumphantly. "You don't like?"

Ariana looked around the small, neat living area. A love seat littered with embroidered pillows sat perpendicular to the doorway, flanked on either side by mahogany side tables. A brown wing chair, matching ottoman, and low coffee table piled with neatly arranged books—*Miss Manners' Guide to Domestic Tranquility* and *The Little Book of Etiquette*—were the only other pieces of furniture that could fit in the room. Every surface in sight was covered with crocheted lace doilies, and half the throw pillows featured Siamese cats.

She tossed Noelle's tank top over an ugly needlepoint pillow stitched with the words WHAT PART OF "MEOW" DON'T YOU UNDERSTAND?

"Mrs. Lattimer is going to murder us," she said. The Billings housemother was notoriously private about her apartment. Before today, Ariana had only caught the briefest glimpses inside it, and only when she happened to be walking by as Mrs. Lattimer was stepping in or out.

"Only if she finds out we were here," Thomas replied. He swiped a doily from the back of the couch and draped it over his arm. "Welcome to Chez Lattimer, Billings House's fine dining experience."

"Seriously, Thomas. Maybe we should try someplace else."

Breaking into Billings was one thing. Breaking into the housemother's locked apartment upped their misdemeanor to a felony.

"Where else are we going to go?" Thomas asked, crossing his arms over his chest.

Ariana bit her lip. For a moment she considered just calling Headmaster Cox, telling him they were here. But then she thought about the assembly of the day before—how he'd said there'd be no exceptions. She realized with a heavy sigh that she and Thomas had already broken too many rules. Thomas was right. There was nowhere. The other remaining students were using the cafeteria, so pilfering food from the kitchen was not an option.

"Before you answer, allow me to show you one of Chez Lattimer's most tempting features." He reached for the thermostat dial on the wall and turned. "Wait for it. . . ." The sound of the ancient pipes screeching in the wall made Ariana jump.

"Heat!" she said happily. She felt as if her bones had been frozen for days.

"Heat," Thomas confirmed.

"This Chez Lattimer is growing on me." Ariana walked over to the tiny kitchen area and sat down on one of stools at the counter. "So, what are your specials?"

Thomas shrugged as he stepped onto the white linoleum floor. "Your guess is as good as mine." He opened a few cabinets. "Let's see. On the menu today, we have brown rice, pancake mix, or Metamucil."

"Wow. Everything sounds so good," Ariana deadpanned. "Surprise me."

"Pancakes it is."

Thomas rooted around the kitchen until he found the requisite ingredients, plus measuring cups, a griddle, and a bowl. He laid it all out on the counter and got to work.

"You know how to cook?" Ariana smiled. She liked the idea that she was learning something new about him.

"How hard is it to follow directions?" he replied.

Ariana watched as he measured the mix in a dry measuring cup and the oil and milk in a liquid measuring cup. A boy would only know the difference if he'd cooked before—Thomas was trying to hide the fact that he knew what he was doing.

"So you've never made these before," she challenged.

His back to her, Thomas paused in his stirring. "Okay, fine. You caught me," he said over his shoulder. "I can do pancakes and grilled cheese."

"Interesting specialties," Ariana said.

"Yeah, well, when I was a kid we didn't really do dinners together as a family and the maid was always making, like, fish with mango chutney, so I used to sneak back into the kitchen and make what I wanted."

"Pancakes and grilled cheese," Ariana said with a smile.

"Exactly."

Ariana understood. It was just like her twelfth birthday when she'd had to plan and throw herself a party because her dad was away and her mother was in one of her states. Sometimes you just had to learn to do these things for yourself. She wondered what had broken Thomas's family. Had it been anything like what happened to hers? A philandering father and a mother who wasn't all there even *before* he broke her heart?

"You never mentioned why you're not going home for Christmas," Ariana said. She watched as Thomas concentrated on the mixing bowl.

"City's too crowded over the holidays," he said quickly. Defensively.

"Thomas," Ariana said.

He glanced up, and their eyes locked. The vulnerability, the pain that she had seen in passing flashes, was there, written in his expression. But this time, it didn't disappear. It only intensified the longer she held his gaze. Only sharpened the deeper she looked.

A lump rose in the back of her throat, and she bit the inside of her cheek. She'd seen that kind of pain before. Staring at her reflection in the mirror of a hospital bathroom. Wondering what unforgivable thing she'd done in life to deserve a family like hers. Instantly hating herself for the thought.

He was silent for a while. "Let's just say Christmas Eve is not fun at the Pearson home. Unless you're big on drunken parental throw-downs."

"Oh," Ariana said. "Has it always been like that?"

"Pretty much since birth," Thomas said with a grim smile. "What about you? Why would you rather spend Christmas with the Sticks-Up-Their-Asses?"

Ariana smirked. "Kind of a long nickname for 'the Ryans.'"

"I'm working on it," Thomas replied. He ran some water over his fingers, then flicked them toward the heated griddle. Water droplets popped and sizzled across the surface. He even knew how to test for the right temperature. "Your parents fighters, too?"

"No." Ariana took a deep breath and sighed, letting the familiar heaviness of family thoughts settle around her. "Worse. They don't speak. Ever. Even when they're in the same room. She just looks at him with this pathetic longing and he completely ignores her presence."

"Well, silence is good," Thomas offered.

"Not this kind of silence," Ariana said sadly, looking down at her hands.

Thomas turned away for a moment and stirred the pancake batter. Ariana let the rhythmic sound of the whisk lull her.

"I never really thought about it as a kid," Thomas said finally.

"Thought about what?"

"The way things were. How they screamed at each other if they

were ever around each other for more than twenty minutes. How at
the end of every meal, they ended up passed out in different rooms.
And then, one Christmas Eve when we were really young, they were
out of town on business. Tokyo or some shit. And so my brother
and I—"

"Blake?"

He nodded. "We went over to a friend's house for dinner. And
it was like something was off. The dad wasn't screaming. The mom
wasn't crying."

Thomas poured the batter onto the hot griddle and a frantic
sizzling sound filled the room.

"Now you know why I like the Sticks-Up-Their-Asses," Ariana
said.

"*They're* normal?" Thomas asked skeptically. He put the bowl
down on the counter. "I find that hard to believe."

"Way more normal than I'm used to."

Thomas finished up with the pancakes in silence, then flipped
them onto two separate plates and slid them onto the countertop. He
sat down on the stool next to Ariana's, his elbow grazing hers. Neither
of them pulled away.

"Syrup?" Ariana said with a smile.

"As you wish," Thomas replied, handing it over to her atop his
forearm as if it were a bottle of wine.

Ariana poured a splash of syrup onto her stack and cut a perfect
triangle out of it. Meanwhile, Thomas grabbed the bottle, doused
his pancakes, and used his knife and fork to decimate them into

a thousand tiny pieces before shoveling a whole forkful into his mouth.

"So were your parents always like that?" he asked after he swallowed.

Ariana's food turned to cement in her stomach. She had never told anyone about her mom. Not even Noelle. She had never wanted to. Never felt she could. It felt disloyal . . . and embarrassing. She lowered her fork and wiped her fingers with her napkin systematically, one by one.

"You can't tell me anything that would shock me," Thomas said matter-of-factly. "Trust me."

Ariana looked over at him. He stared back, his gaze unwavering. Open. Suddenly she felt as if she could tell him the whole truth. His family was screwed up, too. Not like the Ryans. Or even the Langes, who did love each other, even if they had odd ways of showing it.

"You have to swear you won't tell anyone," she said.

"Who would I tell?" Thomas replied.

He had no interest in gossip. That was what he was telling her. He was above that. And she believed him. Ariana took a deep breath, clutched her arm, and let go.

"My mother has been in and out of mental hospitals since before I can remember."

She glanced at him for his reaction. He didn't even blink.

"So growing up, it was mostly my dad and me," Ariana went on. "My mom was only home here and there."

"No brothers and sisters?" he asked.

Ariana's fingers clutched her arm more tightly, but she didn't answer. She had no interest in going there.

"So anyway, when my mom was home, everything was always great for the first couple of days. She would cook and play games with me and just be this . . . this kind of light," Ariana said, staring off. "Sometimes it lasted longer than others, but sooner or later she would always come back down."

"Depression?" Thomas asked, taking a bite of his pancake mash.

"Serious depression," Ariana confirmed. "She'd lock the bedroom door and nobody was allowed in. My dad would always try, but he got more and more frustrated. He started disappearing for days and weeks at a time. Luckily I had a nanny to take care of me. Otherwise . . ."

"What would any of us have done without our nannies?" Thomas joked, trying to lighten the mood.

"Anyway, my mother would always get him to come home with threats," Ariana continued. She tore her paper napkin in half, then in quarters. Perfectly symmetrical little squares.

"Threats?" Thomas asked.

"She'd threaten to . . . you know. . . ." She looked at Thomas. He stared back. He was going to make her say it.

"Kill herself," she said quietly. She tore the napkin again. Eights, then sixteenths, and on and on. The pancakes on her plate had soaked up all the syrup and were turning cold. "And then, one day when I was nine and he'd stayed away for over a month . . . she finally did it."

"Your mother committed suicide?" Thomas blurted. Then he blushed, realizing his faux pas.

"No! No. Well, she tried," Ariana explained.

And just like that, she saw it again. Her mother's seemingly life-less body, curled up in the fetal position on the bathroom rug. The stark orange pills against the white tile floor. Her blond hair spilling out in a perfect halo around her head. Ariana saw it all, and suddenly she felt numb.

"It was the last day of school before Christmas break," she said flatly. Her voice had gone monotone. Detached. It was the only way she could get through the memory. "I'm the one who found her. Called nine-one-one. The doctor said if I'd gotten there even five minutes later . . ."

She heard herself screaming for her mother over and over again. Saw herself hysterically crying into the phone.

"How'd she do it?" Thomas asked. He'd stopped eating.

The question brought her back. "Vicodin. Washed it down with a bottle of vintage wine my dad bought her on their honeymoon," she said, and forced a smirk. "You have to give her points for dramatic flair."

"No shit," Thomas said with a short laugh. "Wow. You must really hate Christmas."

"With a passion," Ariana said.

Her insides felt shaky, but she was glad she'd told Thomas. Her family, her past . . . it wasn't a secret anymore. Something to feel ashamed of. She had told someone and the world hadn't come to an end.

"Still, I wanted to go home and see my mom, but she really wanted me to be with Daniel, so—" She stopped herself.

Thomas looked down at his plate for a second. When he looked up again, his eyes seemed to be a deeper blue than they had been seconds before.

"What about you?" Thomas asked.

"What about me?"

"You said your mom wants you to be with Daniel. But what about you? What do you want?"

Ariana blinked. No one had ever asked her that before. How was it possible that he was the first?

"I . . ." Her voice faltered. "It's . . . complicated."

"Complicated? You either like the guy or you don't. That's the opposite of complicated."

The challenge in his voice set Ariana on edge. "It's not that simple," she replied. "My mother . . . she lives through me. She's *so* proud of me, of my life here. . . . If I ever ended things with Daniel, or got expelled, she would just . . ."

She couldn't finish her thought. Couldn't bear to imagine what would happen. And it would be all her fault. All. Her. Fault.

"That's why I have to go to Vermont," she finished. "I don't have a choice."

"But that's not fair." Thomas was incredulous. "You shouldn't have to live your whole life for her. Doesn't she want you to be happy?"

"Yes, but she believes Easton and Billings and Daniel are the things that will make me happy. And they should." Her voice was getting higher and higher as she spoke. "I mean, they *do*. He's a great guy, and he loves me."

Thomas laughed cruelly. "Daniel Ryan doesn't love anyone but himself."

"You don't know anything," Ariana said, stacking her napkin pieces on the counter. "Why else would he be ready to lose his virgini—"

Thomas gaped at her.

"Wait a minute, wait a minute. Daniel Ryan told you he was a virgin?" he blurted.

Ariana felt her face flaming. "He *is* a virgin."

Thomas's eyes danced merrily, and suddenly it felt like the room was growing warmer. The condescending way he was looking at her, like she was naïve. Stupid. Her blood boiled in her veins. In her mind's eye she saw herself picking up the heavy griddle and slamming the back of Thomas's bent head with it, just to get that look out of his eye.

"Stop looking at me like that!" she said, standing. Her fingers twitched.

"I'm not. . . ." Thomas replied, his eyes serious again. "I'm just . . . I can't believe he told you that. And I can't believe you bought it."

Ariana's blood began to cool.

"I didn't buy anything. It's the truth," Ariana said firmly. "Not that it's any of your business."

"You just made it my business," Thomas said, standing. "Let's go."

"Go where?" Ariana didn't move a muscle.

"I'm going to prove to you that he's lying," Thomas said lightly. "Unless you're scared to know the truth."

Ariana lifted her chin. "I'm not scared of anything."

"Good. Then I propose a bet," Thomas said, picking his coat up off the couch where he'd tossed it earlier.

"What kind of bet?" Ariana asked.

"I bet I can prove that Daniel Ryan is no virgin," Thomas said, looking down at her. "If I'm wrong, I'll . . ."

"Come back here and clean this mess up on your own?" Ariana suggested, though the very idea of leaving it behind made her skin crawl.

"Fine, and if you're wrong, you have to kiss me again," Thomas said.

"Very creative," Ariana said, rolling her eyes.

"Men are a simple breed," Thomas joked.

"Fine," Ariana said. "Let's get this over with."

She pushed past him and yanked her own coat off the sofa. She knew Daniel would never lie to her. Not about something this big. And after the way he'd demeaned her, she couldn't wait to wipe that cocky smirk off Thomas Pearson's face.

NEAR MISS

Thomas shoved open the back door of Billings and they were both blasted in the face with ice and snow. Ariana could hardly see three feet in front of her.

"Come on. I'll make sure you don't blow away." Thomas had to shout to be heard over the whistling wind. He offered her his ungloved hand.

She took it with her gloved one, telling herself it was just for survival purposes and for no other reason, and together they set out into the storm. The snow had piled up so high it kissed the frames of the first-floor windows. As they took their first steps, their legs sank down and the snow came right up to their knees. Ariana cringed as the cold soaked her fresh pair of jeans. Sharp gusts of wind blew the falling snow in dizzying circles around them.

Ariana's eyes burned. Tears spilled down her cheeks when she blinked.

"Maybe this was a bad idea," she yelled. She turned around and stared longingly through the window into Mrs. Lattimer's apartment. The memory of the cozy little kitchen disappeared with the next blast of wind.

"Just keep going," Thomas replied.

They trudged the rest of the way without trying to speak. When they finally reached the back door of Ketlar, they huddled under the overhang, out of the way of the ice and snow. Ariana took a deep breath. Her hair was soaked, her nose was running, and her ears felt as if they were about to break off.

"That wasn't so bad." Thomas's eyes looked gray against the eerie, snowy sky. The dark clouds above had a yellowish tinge, making it impossible to tell that it was just past noon.

Ariana simply stared him down, thinking about Noelle, all cozy in New York, probably eating mahi-mahi at Fred's at Barneys with her parents, and the Ryans sitting together in front of a roaring fireplace in Vermont. All things she could be doing were she not stuck in this blizzard. She pushed her matted hair behind her shoulders. "Let's just get inside."

Thomas reached for the door and Ariana saw a dark figure move out of the corner of her eye. Suddenly Thomas yanked her inside. Together they ducked below the window in the Ketlar front door and Ariana held her breath.

"Who the hell is that?" Thomas whispered. "No one's staying on this side of campus."

Ariana inched up and, ignoring Thomas's whispered pleas to stay down, peeked out the window. A tall, lithe figure, hunched against the wind moved slowly by, following the general route of the cobblestone pathway that was covered by the snow. Jet black hair whipped wildly in the wind.

"It's just Isobel," Ariana whispered, dropping down again. "I don't think she saw us."

Thomas breathed a sigh of relief. "What the hell is she doing back here?"

"She's here for a week while her parents are on vacation."

"Isobel Bautista couldn't figure out another vacation plan?" Thomas raised an eyebrow. "Sounds like an excuse to me."

Ariana shrugged and tried to slow her breathing. Her lungs felt like they were filled with shards of glass. "We have to be more careful. If the wrong stay-behind student catches us, we're screwed."

"I know." Thomas stood and grabbed Ariana's hands to pull her up. "I can't get caught. My parents will disinherit me."

"Yeah. Mine too," Ariana said dryly. She pressed her hands on either side of her nose in an attempt to warm it. It didn't work.

"No. Seriously." Thomas's voice echoed in the empty Ketlar lobby. "One more strike, and I'm cut out of the will. Everything goes to Blake."

Ariana stared at Thomas in disbelief. "They'd do that?"

Thomas nodded. "They warned me after the last time Headmaster Cox called them. Some freshman told the Wesley advisor that I sold him Adderall."

"Did you?" she asked, already knowing the answer.

"Ungrateful prick," Thomas muttered. He turned and strode over to the elevator as if he hadn't just admitted to being a drug dealer. "Let's go," he threw over his shoulder. "You've got a bet to lose."

THE BET

"I can't believe I'm doing this," Ariana said, standing outside the door to Daniel's dorm room. "He'd kill me."

"Kill you, huh? Sounds like a winner," Thomas teased.

Ariana shot him a look of death and shoved the door open. Piles of dirty sports uniforms, back issues of *ESPN* magazine, and protein bar wrappers covered the floor. His dresser exploded with clothes, and a bowl of half-eaten cereal sat on his desk.

"This is nasty," Thomas announced, eyeing a pair of grass- and mud-stained shorts on Daniel's bed. "Even for a dude."

"He doesn't have a lot of time to clean," Ariana said, wrinkling her nose as she stepped over a lacrosse helmet.

"Oh, right. Because he's so busy with all his clubs and teams and being First every semester. Message received," Thomas replied.

Embarrassed that he'd read her so easily, Ariana turned away and automatically started picking up after Daniel, folding clothes that looked clean and swiping the dirty ones into his hamper. As she was trying to shove a T-shirt inside, Thomas pulled it away from her and dumped the entire contents out in front of the closet doors.

"What are you doing?" Ariana wailed.

Thomas rifled through the clothes. "Proof enough?" he asked, lifting a lacy camisole from the mess. "Either your boy is getting some on the side, or he likes to play dress-up. Either way, you lose."

"That's mine." Ariana smiled, snatching the cami away from him. "Glad you like it, though."

"Huh." Thomas eyed the camisole in her hands, then shifted his gaze to her body, letting his eyes wander.

"Strike one," she said quickly, stuffing the flimsy garment into her pocket. "Give up?"

"No way," Thomas scoffed. "I'm just getting started."

He ambled over to Daniel's desk, opening and slamming the doors one after the other. Finally he tossed a bunch of books on the floor and a slow grin surfaced.

"Score." He took a seat on the desk and pulled Daniel's laptop onto his lap. "Password?"

She shrugged. "No idea," she said lightly. She crossed the room and leaned back against the desk next to him. "Sorry."

"Oh, come on," he protested. "You don't know your own boy-friend's password?"

"I told you, I trust him. And he trusts me."

Lie.

"Yeah?" Thomas raised his brows skeptically.

"As a general rule, I don't go snooping around in his personal stuff."

"*Didn't*," Thomas corrected her. "You *didn't* go snooping around in his personal stuff. Until now." He paused, drumming his fingers on the desk. "What's his lacrosse number?"

"Twenty-nine," she replied. "But that's way too obvious."

Still. Thomas typed *Ryan29* in the password prompt box. *Invalid password* flashed on the screen. *Daniel29*, *DRyan29*, and *LAX29* elicited the same response.

"Aw." Ariana pouted. "Strike two."

She lifted the cereal bowl onto the shelf above the desk and sat down next to Thomas. A strange sensation spread through her body. Relief? Not possible. She hadn't expected Thomas to find anything. Daniel had never given her a reason not to trust him. And if he shouldn't trust her anymore, she did trust him. There was no reason for them to be there, going through his personal stuff. Her hair was still damp, but suddenly she felt like she needed another shower.

"Okay," she announced, tapping her fingernails against the desk. "You gave it a shot. Now let's get out of here." The sound of her own nails on the oak surface made her even jumpier. "Let's go. Please."

"You have to give me a fair chance to win the bet," Thomas muttered. "All right. We'll try something easier. What's his birthday?"

She sighed impatiently. "August twelfth."

Thomas typed in Daniel's birthday. It didn't work. Ariana jumped off the desk and picked up Daniel's books from the floor. "Come on.

You've got some dishes to do." She arranged the books haphazardly across the desk, even though it pained her not to leave a neat stack, and turned for the door.

"Wait. Give me one more shot." Thomas bent over the keyboard.

"No, we're leaving." She chose to ignore the dog-eared issue of *Maxim* next to her foot and focused instead on the screen as Thomas typed the word *password* into the prompt box.

Welcome, Daniel Ryan! flashed on the screen, and a picture of Daniel holding his lacrosse stick glowed behind his desktop icons. Her heart sank.

"Unbelievable." Thomas smirked. "You're dating a tool, you know that?'

"Shut up," Ariana replied through her teeth.

"We'll try his IM conversations first," he said, skillfully clicking his way through Daniel's saved conversations.

"For the record, this is wrong," she announced, even though her heart was pounding from the intrigue. Morbid curiosity was definitely getting the better of her. "We shouldn't be doing this."

"It's a little late for that kind of talk," he replied, scanning the list of conversations. He opened one and skimmed it, laughing quietly to himself. "Oh, this is good."

"What?" Ariana's heart thumped. He looked like he'd just hit the jackpot.

"Just read."

Thomas shifted the laptop screen in her direction. Her heart sped up as she read the first lines of the conversation.

RyanLAX (8:07 P.M.): U there? Come over

Angel01 (8:08 P.M.): Can't. Too much work for tomorrow.
Tomorrow night if you're good.

RyanLAX (8:11 P.M.): Any way to convince u?

Angel01 (8:13 P.M.): You have something in mind?

RyanLAX (8:15 P.M.): Come over and find out

Angel01 (8:18 P.M.): Need a hint first

RyanLAX (8:19 P.M.): Hint: u won't need ur clothes

Angel01 (8:21 P.M.): Good thing I just got out of the shower ;)

She felt Thomas's eyes on her, and her face warmed.

"That's enough," she said slowly, exiting out of the conversation. "I don't need to read any more." She pushed the laptop screen toward Thomas and looked away.

Thomas shifted. "Listen, Ariana," he began. "It's better for you to know now before you—"

Ariana laughed. "Could you be any more gullible? I don't need to read any more because I'm Angel-zero-one!"

Thomas's eyes were wide. "So you *are* a naughty girl."

Ariana blushed. "Are you ready to admit it yet? Just admit Daniel's not a liar and we can go."

"Not even close," Thomas replied. He opened up a couple of files from the desktop and scanned the contents. Ariana watched him, and after a few clicks of the mouse, she saw his face change. He paused, and his eyes flickered with interest. Ariana's fingers clenched along with her stomach.

"What?"

When Thomas looked at her, the disgust and pity were clear in his eyes.

"Nothing. I can't find anything. Let's get out of here."

Thomas started to lower the screen, but she reached over and blocked him. Her heart pounded an erratic beat. There was something on that screen.

"Give it to me," she said, wrenching the computer from his hands.

Thomas made a futile grab for it. "Ariana—"

She blinked at the glowing screen in confusion. The spreadsheet Daniel used to keep track of his lacrosse stats was open. She scanned the familiar columns: goals, attempts, assists. A second tab, titled *scores*, was attached to the spreadsheet.

"It's his lacrosse stats. Big deal," she said, hovering the cursor over the *scores* tab.

"I wouldn't click that," Thomas said, scratching the back of his neck.

So, of course, Ariana had to click it. Instantly a new spreadsheet filled the screen, but it wasn't the spreadsheet she was expecting. The left column was filled with girls' names. Some she recognized, and some she didn't. The right column was filled with dates, the first in August of Daniel's freshman year, four years before.

"I don't understand. What . . ."

Then she saw the final name in the column. *Ariana Osgood*. The entry next to it read, *Senior year Christmas break*.

All of the oxygen was sucked right out of Ariana's lungs. Her chest tightened. This was a list of girls that Daniel had slept with, and she was next in line. He wasn't a virgin. He had been sleeping with every girl on campus and then some since he arrived at Easton. Even worse, everyone must have known it. Everyone knew what a naïve idiot she was. The guy who said he loved her, said he wanted her to be his first, had humiliated her in front of the entire school. Lied to her for the entire year they'd been together. She checked the dates again. He'd slept with two other girls *while they were dating.*

I'm such a loser. Such a stupid, stupid, loser. He used me. I let him use me.

"Ariana? Are you okay?"

They're all laughing at me. All of them. Laughing at me behind my back.

Ariana started to tremble again. The computer shook in her hands. She was nothing but a number on a spreadsheet. A nothing. A blip. She was worthless. She grabbed her arm, her nails cutting deep grooves in her sweater. *I may as well just kill myself now. No one would miss me. No one would care.*

"He's a jackass," Thomas said quietly. "He doesn't deserve you."

Ariana looked up at Thomas and everything seemed to snap into place. Someone would care. Thomas would care. He'd just said it himself. She was too good for Daniel. *Thomas* thought she was worth something.

Ariana dropped the computer. It slammed on the floor and died with a sickening *zip* and a flash of the screen, but she didn't even care. She grabbed Thomas's coat and pulled him toward her, pressing her lips, her body against his. Nothing that had stood between them before mattered now. She felt a weight lifting from her shoulders as he kissed her back.

Daniel didn't deserve her. . . . He didn't deserve her. . . . She was done belonging to him.

Ariana grabbed Thomas by the collar and stripped his coat down his arms. He flung it to the floor as her hands moved to his shirt. They were no longer trembling. As her fingers unbuttoned his shirt, she was moving with a steady purpose.

Screw Daniel Ryan. Screw him and his perfect family and his perfect life. "You sure?" Thomas murmured as she pushed his shirt off his bare shoulders. His body was perfect. Taut and lean and tan.

"A bet's a bet," she smiled, kissing his neck, running her fingers over his chest. "And I'm not a sore loser."

"We should get out of here," Thomas breathed. "Go back to my room."

He picked up his coat and started for the door, holding her hand in his.

"I want to do it here." She pointed meaningfully to Daniel's unmade bed and pulled her sweater off over her head. "He deserves it."

Thomas smiled and dropped his coat back on the floor. He moved on top of her quickly, leaning her back into the familiar pillows. He would die if he knew what she was doing right now. He would just die.

"I like the way you think, naughty girl," Thomas said, hovering over her.

With a grin, Ariana pulled Thomas's warm body down on top of her. And even though she'd sworn to Daniel Ryan that she would never lose her virginity in his dorm room, that's exactly what she did.

It almost felt like a dream, like it hadn't really happened. Ariana relaxed into Thomas's strong chest and closed her eyes, replaying the series of images in her mind like a silent movie on a projector screen. After their first go in Daniel's room, they had sneaked back to Thomas's room and started all over again. This time, it had been more romantic. More tender. Wearing nothing but his boxers, Thomas had kissed her in front of his door, then let her inside before pulling her sweater off over her head. She was naked underneath, but in the dim light of his room, she felt totally safe. Secure. They had made love again, more slowly this time, and Ariana had recorded every detail in her mind. Every touch, every kiss, every inch of him.

This was monumental. It was a day she would never forget. She wanted to remember every single thing.

Now the sun had set outside and the room was dark save for the light from the candles Thomas had lit before drifting off to sleep.

Behind her, he shifted slightly and she sank back toward him on his bed, smiling at the intimacy of it all. Thomas was nothing like Daniel. He would never leave her feeling vulnerable like Daniel had. Her mother would understand that. After what Daniel had done, she would have to.

Shifting uncomfortably in Thomas's single bed, she realized her fleur-de-lis necklace was digging into her collarbone. She brought her fingers to her chest. The necklace had left a deep imprint of the flower in her skin.

"You okay?" Thomas said groggily. He kissed the top of her head, and she raised her face to his. Flickering light from the candles on his desk bathed them in warmth.

"Better than okay." She smiled, tracing the outline of his arm with her fingertip. The sound of her own voice surprised her. There wasn't a trace of self-consciousness, of worry, in her words. Or her body.

Ariana Osgood was finally calm. Perfectly, blissfully calm.

"Me too," he murmured, stroking her hair. He looked into her eyes with a fixed gaze, concentrating only on her. As if nothing else in the world could possibly matter to him more. As if nothing could tear him away from her. Not Daniel, or the threat of being expelled, or their dysfunctional families. He wanted to be there with her. Completely.

She felt herself melting into him. The tension that had built up inside her over the past hours—over the past several years, really—had vanished, leaving her weightless. Free. Her breathing slow and even. She wondered if this was what happy felt like.

"Pretty quiet," Thomas observed, his fingers trailing down her bare back. Goosebumps rose along her skin.

"Just thinking," Ariana said softly, resting in the crook of his arm. She had imagined what this moment would be like for so long that she could hardly believe it actually happened. She had always fantasized about meeting the perfect guy, about falling perfectly in love. Being the heroine of her own novel. Living Happily Ever After.

But Thomas wasn't perfect at all. He was sarcastic and messy and he said the wrong things. But he knew what it was like to grow up the way she had. And he didn't fault her for it.

"Thinking about?" Thomas prompted her.

"About how this is what I need." It was exactly what she meant, and she felt safe enough to say it. No masks, no pretending.

She kissed him lightly on the lips, then on the nose. He tasted like maple syrup. "Mmm, breakfast," she laughed, pulling away from him and licking her lips.

Thomas grinned. "You taste pretty good too."

He showered her with a series of quick, biting kisses that trailed from her lips to her neck. She pushed him away, and he fought back, pressing his hand against the back of her neck and pulling her into him.

"Don't think you can get away so easy," he said into her ear. "Now that I've got you, I'm not letting go of you anytime soon."

A pleasant warmth engulfed Ariana's heart. He loved her. She knew he loved her.

"You better not."

Sitting up, she tried to flash him a menacing stare, but the amused glint in his eyes just made her burst out laughing all over again.

"Oh, yeah?" he challenged her, slipping his hands around her waist. "What are you gonna do?"

"You don't want to find out," she warned him playfully. "Believe me."

"Ooh," he laughed. "I'm so scared of big, bad Ariana."

He wrapped his arms tighter around her and pulled her into him. Ariana smiled and drifted off to sleep. Perfectly, blissfully calm. Seconds later, the loud shriek of a siren yanked her right out of a shapeless dream.

"What the fuck?" Thomas shouted.

Ariana's heart was in her throat. "It's the fire alarm!"

Thomas tripped out of bed, fished a sweatshirt out of his laundry hamper, and pulled it on. Somehow, Ariana found her jeans underneath the bed. The damp denim clung to her skin, and her heart raced as she struggled to zip them up. She shoved her feet into her boots, yanked her coat from Thomas's desk chair, and quickly blew out all the candles.

"We have to get out of here." Thomas reached for her hand and pulled her toward the door. "Come on!"

"No!" She pulled back. "We can't go out that way. They'll be coming to check the dorm any second. By the time we get through the snowdrifts outside they'll see us!" Her head was starting to throb. She couldn't think with the sound of that alarm blaring in her head.

"We don't have a choice!" Thomas yelled. "If we stay here, they'll catch us anyway. I can't get expelled, Ariana, I can't!" His eyes were wild, his voice hoarse over the screeching alarm.

"I know!" she screamed. He was right. They couldn't leave, and they couldn't stay.

They were trapped.

THE LEAP

"We have to take the window."

"Are you crazy?" Ariana blurted. "We're on the second floor!"

"So what are we gonna do? Just give up?" Thomas demanded.

"No," Ariana said. If there was one thing she would never do, it was give up. Her mother had given up. And as much as Ariana loved her, she had promised herself she would never be like her mother.

"Then help me," Thomas said.

He slipped his fingers into the grooves at the bottom of the window and Ariana did the same. With a deep breath, they threw their weight against it. The warped wood stayed frozen in place.

"Shit." Thomas turned around and eyed the doorway nervously.

"Come on! Let's try it again."

He rejoined Ariana. "Okay. One, two, three!" he shouted.

Together they strained at the window. Ariana held her breath and pulled until she felt as if her fingers were going to break off backward.

Then, just when she thought she couldn't take anymore, the window finally gave.

"Let's go!" Thomas turned away as a blast of cold air swept into the room.

Ariana moved cautiously to the window. The blizzard had almost subsided, and only a light, translucent curtain of snowflakes tumbled to the ground below. The snow-capped evergreens at the edge of the woods loomed thick not far from the back door of Ketlar. She took a step back, nearly tripping over Thomas. The icy ground below her looked far, far away.

"I can't." She shook her head. "It's too much of a drop. We have to get out some other way."

"There isn't another way," Thomas said harshly. He gripped her wrist so tightly she winced. "And there's all that snow to break our fall." He straddled the windowsill, bending at the waist to fit through the small opening. "I'll go first."

"Thomas! Don't!"

But he pushed away from the building and fell. Ariana stared after him, imagining his body lying broken and dead on the ground below. But instead, he landed in the soft cushion of snow piled beneath the window. He was fine.

"Come on! You can do it!" he whisper-shouted up to her.

Body trembling, Ariana sat on the edge of the windowsill, her feet still planted on Thomas's floor. One leg at a time, she drew her knees up to her chest. She pivoted her body and lowered her legs outside the window. The sight of Thomas on the ground blurred beneath her.

"I can't." The thought of her body free-falling from the window made her skin prickle with fear.

"I'm right here. Come on, Ariana," he pleaded. "Jump."

She screwed her eyes shut and hesitated.

I can't do it. I can't do it. I can't—

"I won't let anything happen to you," Thomas said.

Ariana's heart flipped in her chest. Right. He would protect her. He loved her. She looked down at him, took a deep breath, and shoved away from the window. Icy wind slipped past her and she landed, hard, against Thomas's body. The sound of bone on bone cracked in the air as they both hit the snow.

"You okay?" Thomas winced. His face was contorted in pain. Ariana struggled her way off of him and knelt next to his body in the snow.

"You're hurt."

"I'm fine," he said through gritted teeth. "Really."

Guilt seeped into her skin faster than the wet snow. "You're not. And it's my fault," she insisted. She lowered her numb fingers to his ankle, and he tensed in pain. "We have to—"

"Right now what we have to do is get out of here," he interrupted. He scanned the back edge of Ketlar and nodded at a huge evergreen that loomed over the far corner of the dorm, at a diagonal from the back door. "Over there," he said tersely.

Silently, she pulled his arm over her shoulder and helped him to his feet. He dropped his head toward her neck, his jaw tensed. The weight of his body scared her. If he couldn't take care of himself, he definitely couldn't take care of her.

Thomas lifted one foot off the ground and they moved quickly along the dorm to the tree, about thirty feet from the rear of Ketlar. She helped him around the thick trunk, and they leaned against the jagged bark on the side facing the woods.

Thomas closed his eyes. "The snow," he said, curling his hands into fists at his side. "You've got to cover it up so nobody knows we were back there."

The edge to his voice made Ariana cringe. She brushed the snow from Thomas's curls, peering into his eyes. "Thomas," she began, "I'm really—"

"Not your fault," he said, a small smile playing across his lips. "I was stupid enough to stand under a window with a girl jumping out of it. I deserve what I got." He slid down the trunk of the tree, settling onto the ground with a weak laugh. "Now go on, before you get us both expelled."

She hurried along the back of the building and dropped to her knees in the snow, smoothing the spot below Thomas's window where their bodies had landed. She moved backward, running her hands haphazardly over her two footprints and Thomas's single footprint that traced their path to the tree. It wasn't perfect, but it would have to do.

"What the hell was that?" she whispered, collapsing next to him. "Who tripped the alarm? Who would have—"

Thomas reached up and covered her mouth with his hand, shaking his head slowly. Someone was coming. She froze at the faint sound of snow crunching underneath someone's feet.

"Hello?" A familiar voice echoed in the darkness. "Is anyone there?"

The footsteps paused by the back door, not far from their hiding place. Sweat dripped from Ariana's temples and trickled down her flushed cheeks, despite the cold. She turned her head, peeking out from behind the thick trunk.

The slight figure of Dean Marcus, the dean of students, was huddled underneath a full-length gray wool coat. A plaid scarf was wrapped around his neck and a hat was pulled low over his ears, but Ariana recognized his stooped posture and his slow, shuffling walk. Dean Marcus was Headmaster Cox's henchman. The man who was solely responsible for her future at Easton was standing just a few feet away.

Any student who is found to be in violation of these rules will face immediate expulsion. There are no exceptions. None.

It seemed like years ago that she'd heard those words during morning assembly, but now they came rushing back to her, threatening her all over again. If he turned around, he'd see them. But it was too late to move. Ariana closed her eyes, crossed her fingers, and hoped that a man as ancient as Dean Marcus had cataracts.

Just as the dean was about to turn in her direction, the lamps around Ketlar went out with a hissing pop. Everything went dark. The campus suddenly seemed colder. Deserted. Dead.

Ariana clutched Thomas's arm.

"It's just a power failure from the storm," he whispered.

He reached for her hand and interlaced his fingers with hers, squeezing them so tightly that her knuckles ached. His breath was shallow against her neck.

"At least now he can't see us," he whispered.

Beep, beep, beep.

Ariana's heart stopped. Her phone.

"Hello?" Dean Marcus's voice echoed all around him.

Please don't walk over here. Please don't walk over here. Please, please, please. Ariana closed her numb fingers over her phone, muting the beeps.

The dean turned from the doorway. He was facing them now, squinting into the darkness. She waited for him to call their names. Waited for him to tell her that her life was over. That they were both expelled.

But he just sighed and turned away, leaving a jagged path behind him in the snow.

"Oh my God," Ariana sighed, relief flooding her frozen body.

"Who the hell is texting you?" Thomas demanded.

Ariana flipped her phone open.

Daniel: Ariana, this is unacceptable. Hope you're ready to beg for forgiveness. WHERE THE HELL ARE YOU????

She turned the phone around to show the screen to Thomas. All at once, her stomach heaved. She swallowed repeatedly to keep from throwing up. Her skin burned in spite of the cold, and she tried to breathe.

"What an ass," Thomas said. "Does he not know what's going on out here?"

Ariana groaned. "Don't you get it, Thomas? He *knows* where I am. He knows what we've been doing. He's just trying to torture me."

"You don't actually still think that he's here on campus." It wasn't a question, and she didn't answer. "You're being paranoid, Ariana." But he didn't sound as sure as he once had.

"Am I?" she retorted. "He didn't even acknowledge the message I left him letting him know I was on my way."

Ariana's nerves crackled beneath her skin, and suddenly she heard her mother's voice on the morning she'd tried to kill herself.

You never know what people are capable of until they're pushed to their edge, Ariana.

Grimacing, Thomas drew his good knee to his chest. "So? He's clearly a self-centered prick. He's probably just ignoring it."

Thomas shivered in the darkness. In the dim moonlight his skin was ashen. Ariana could have kicked herself for focusing on Daniel when Thomas clearly needed her.

"It doesn't matter right now." She anchored her palms against the tree and pushed herself to standing. There wasn't an inch of her that wasn't soaked. If they didn't get out of there, find someplace warm to sleep, they'd freeze. "We've got to get you something for your ankle."

"I've got some Vicodin in my desk. Second drawer." He paused, closing his eyes. "But I don't want you going in there by yourself. We'll get it later. Let's just get out of here."

"No, I'll go."

She hoped the terror she felt at the thought of returning to Thomas's room alone didn't show. What if Daniel was there, waiting for her? But Thomas needed her. She reached into his jacket pocket, fishing out his lighter.

"Ariana," he protested weakly.

"Don't go anywhere," she said dryly.

"Hilarious."

You can do this, Ariana. Do it for Thomas. As she sprinted for the back door, she couldn't push the thought of Daniel from her mind, couldn't stop wondering if he had been on campus the whole time. Watching her every move with Thomas. He could have seen everything. He could have watched as she lost her virginity to another guy.

And, Ariana reminded herself, if there was one thing Daniel Ryan hated, it was losing.

EASY

The biting chill in Thomas's room hit her the second she walked through the door. Snow had drifted in through the open window, and the hollow sound of the wind rattling the glass made her skin crawl. She paused in the doorway, taking a slow, deep breath. She could do this. All she had to do was find Thomas's pills. She'd be out of Ketlar and back with him in less than a minute. Everything was going to be fine. They were both going to be fine.

She held the lighter in front of her, moving slowly across Thomas's room to his desk. The weak flame cast a shallow light over the items scattered across the surface: the pencils, the chewed-up ballpoint pen, the empty Captain Morgan's bottle.

She opened the first drawer. Gum, old magazines, highlighters, and an article from the *Easton Academy Chronicle* about the soccer team's performance in a local tournament. She stared at the crinkled black-and-white picture of the team huddled together on the field. Thomas grinned back at her, cradling the ball under his arm. Ariana fought the urge to fold the photo up and put it in her pocket. There would be plenty of time for photo ops after this weekend.

Second drawer. The sooner you find the pills, the sooner you can get out of here. She slammed the top drawer shut and reached for the handle below it. Two heavy packages of computer paper were stuffed in the second drawer. Nothing else.

The metal tip of the lighter was starting to warm, and she winced against the heat. Mind racing, she tried to think like Thomas. If she had a reputation for selling drugs, if she'd come close to expulsion several times, where would she hide her pills? He'd told her they were in the second drawer. Could he have made a mistake?

She pulled the heavy packages of paper from the drawer. Nothing but smooth wood underneath. She ran her fingers over the bottom of the drawer, and the wood tilted slightly under her touch. She pressed the far edge of the drawer, harder this time, and the edge closest to her tilted upward, revealing a stash of prescription bottles underneath. Jackpot. Only Thomas would think to equip his desk drawer with a false bottom to hide his drugs.

She lowered the lighter over the bottles and scanned the labels. Ritalin, Adderall, Percoset, Vicodin. And no two names on the prescription labels were alike. Thomas was running a black market pharmacy from his second desk drawer. The old Ariana would have been horrified, but the new Ariana just stuffed the bottle of Vicodin into her coat pocket and shoved the drawer closed. The sound of it slamming made her jump, and a small laugh slipped from her lips. Thomas was right. She was paranoid.

She pushed herself to standing with her free hand, but something on the desk caught her eye. A sheet of paper she hadn't noticed before. Ariana held the flame closer. It was a picture. As the lines and shadows on the page came into focus, her heart seized in her chest and she dropped the lighter.

No. No, no, no, no, no. No.

She shook her head in disbelief at the image in front of her. An image of Thomas and her, kissing in Daniel's room. An image of her hands on Thomas's body, unbuttoning his shirt. Her face wasn't visible, but there was no mistaking her wet blond hair or her stark white coat. Someone had seen them together. Someone had proof.

It wasn't possible. It couldn't be. Bile rose in her throat. This one piece of paper would ruin her. Would ruin them. She let out a low, desperate moan, pressing her forehead against the surface of the desk. She needed Thomas now, more than ever. Needed him to hold her, to tell her that everything would be fine. She couldn't believe that just minutes ago they'd been in bed together, happy. Calm.

Unlike her mother, who had given up on her life, on her husband, Ariana was determined to cling to that feeling of happiness for dear life. But first she had to find the lighter. Stuffing the picture in her back pocket, she dropped to her knees and slid her hands beneath the desk. After a minute, her hands closed around a metal rectangle. The lighter, thank God.

But as she stood, something warm in the bitter cold of Thomas's room slipped across the back of her neck. A warm breath. New electricity surged through her body, and the hairs along her arms prickled. Someone was behind her. Almost touching her in the tarry darkness.

Someone had been waiting for her to find the picture.

Hope you're ready to beg for forgiveness.

Could it be Daniel?

Suddenly it didn't matter who it was. Whoever it was wasn't supposed to be here. And clearly didn't want her here. Instinctively, her hand moved toward the empty rum bottle on the desk. In one swift movement, her fingers closed around its neck, and she brought the bottle down hard against the corner of the desk. The sharp sound of shattering glass cut through the darkness, and she whirled around, swinging the broken bottle wildly in front of her.

A voice cried out in surprise, or pain. She couldn't tell if it was male or female—or if was actually her voice. All she knew was that she had to fight. She sliced the bottle frantically through the air, jabbing this way and that, as she ran for the window, dropping it on the floor in the moment before she jumped.

Seconds later she slammed into the ground, harder this time, landing on her side in the icy snow. Her arm was twisted beneath her, and she groaned as she pulled herself to her feet.

Pulse racing, she looked up at the curtains that were fluttering in Thomas's window. No one was there—at least not anymore. For a moment she just stood there, the snow swirling around her in the darkened campus, and she realized that never in her life—not even when she'd found her mother that awful afternoon—had she been as scared as she was right now.

BLOOD

"Ariana!" Thomas's strained voice echoed in the darkness. No longer comforting, it radiated cold, hard fear.

The frigid air burned her lungs as she hurried toward him. He was slumped against the tree, deflated, his eyes screwed shut. The last bit of color had slipped from his cheeks.

"Someone was . . . There was . . ."

Ariana heaved, collapsing in the snow next to him. She buried her face in Thomas's jacket, inhaling his scent. What she wanted more than anything was his protection. But she knew, deep down, that couldn't keep her safe anymore. He was too weak. And just as afraid as she was.

He slipped his fingers into her hair. "You're okay," he murmured quietly. "You're okay."

She pulled away, wiping the snow from her face with the back of her sleeve. "Someone was in there with me," she managed. "In your room. Waiting for me."

"What?" Thomas was shocked—frightened. "Did you see them?"

She shook her head. "It was dark, and he was behind me, and I couldn't—" Her breath was shallow, and she was starting to get dizzy. She closed her eyes, her voice cracking. "I'm sorry."

She decided not to tell him about the picture. Not yet. Not until she could figure out what to do.

"It's okay," he repeated. "We'll hide out in Drake for a while. Warm up until we can decide what to do next."

"Thomas, we can't," she protested. "Someone will see us."

But even as the words left her mouth, she knew that Thomas was right. He was hurt, and they couldn't stay exposed like this for much longer. Unless they wanted to make the long trek back to Billings and Mrs. Lattimer's apartment—which would be impossible with Thomas in his present condition—it would have to be Drake. It was the only heated dorm on campus. Breaking in was a risk they would have to take.

"We'll go in through the basement," he decided. "But I've gotta take a couple of those pills first." He pulled his hand from her face as she dug through her pocket for the prescription bottle.

"Here." She shook several pills from the bottle into her palm.

He took the pills with his other hand and popped them in his mouth, tilting his head back and swallowing. "Let's get out of here."

Ariana pulled him to his feet, and he leaned against her. They struggled around the side of Ketlar toward Drake. It was extremely slow going with the snow as deep as it was, and his weight seemed to grow heavier as they neared the dorm. Ariana's muscles burned with every step, and her mind raced with thoughts of Daniel. She hadn't wanted to believe that he could hurt her like this, hadn't wanted to think that he could. . . . She shook her head, trying to clear her.

Drake rose up in front of them, looking just as cold and dead as Ketlar had. Even though they wouldn't have electricity, at least they'd have heat. She stopped when they rounded the side of the building, leaning against Drake's frozen exterior. She wasn't sure she had the will to walk another step. She reminded herself that the dorm was heated. *Almost there.* She gritted her teeth and took another step.

"Basement windows are always unlocked," Thomas mumbled. "I've gotten in this way a few times. Never fails." Ariana braced herself against Thomas's deadweight. He had definitely taken too much Vicodin. It wouldn't be long before he was unconscious.

"Just stay with me a little longer," she demanded.

Four large windows, evenly spaced along the back edge of Drake, looked over the dorm basement. She made it to the first window, collapsing against it.

"Think you can hold yourself up while I open the window?"

She lifted Thomas's face to hers. His eyes were half-closed, and a smile played across his lips.

"Thomas," she said sternly.

"Yeah . . ." He nodded.

"Good."

She crouched down in front of the window, pressing her palms against the glass.

"It's warm," she announced, wiping the pane with her sleeve and peering inside. The basement was cluttered with large cardboard boxes stacked to the ceiling and buckets full of cleaning and yard supplies. A large furnace was situated on the other side of the basement, next to the long flight of stairs that led to Drake's first floor.

She gripped the window and tugged it upward. It gave instantly, and a blast of warm air escaped from inside. Surprised, she fell back and landed on her butt.

"Told you," Thomas murmured with a smile. "I know my way around this dorm. Wanna know why?"

"Not really." She dragged a thick pine branch over to the window and wedged it between the window and the windowsill. The opening was almost six feet above the floor. Thomas wouldn't be able to make it without hurting his ankle again. But they didn't have a choice. She slipped through the opening, knees bent, and landed on her feet. The air was musty, and she doubled over in a coughing fit.

"We used to have beer pong tournaments down here. I used to sneak in with a girl named Rebecca," Thomas droned from outside. "I think that's her name." He slid his legs through the window and grinned down at Ariana from his perch above. "That's it. Definitely Rebecca or Lindsay or Paige." He paused. "Or Juliana. We know a Juliana? No. Wait. We know an Ariana."

"Yes, we do," Ariana sighed. "Do you think you can jump?" She took a step back from the window.

"Paige," Thomas mused, his words beginning to slur. "She's kind of a bitch, huh?"

Ariana laughed out loud in spite of herself. "Now, Thomas. Before you're out cold."

"Yeah. Okay." Thomas flipped over on his stomach and eased down slowly. He released his hands from the window and dropped the last few inches to the floor. "How's that?"

"Fine," she said, her face flushing with embarrassment. High as a kite, and he could still figure out a better way in than she could. She guided his hand over her shoulder, and they navigated their way through the cluttered basement. She eyed the narrow staircase that rose up from the right corner of the room, wishing she could stroll up the stairs and into a warm, safe bed.

Instead she had to settle for the hollow space underneath the stairs. Once she'd propped Thomas against the wall, she stopped to look at him. His face was smeared with dark blood.

How had that gotten there? She frantically searched his face and body for cuts, anything. After a moment she rested her face in her hands, defeated, exhausted. Cold. But there was something sticky on her hands. Warm almost.

"Oh my God." She heaved, realizing the blood was coming from her. It was all over her hands, her hair. She tore her coat off, examined her own body for cuts. There were none. But that couldn't be right, unless . . .

The blood wasn't hers.

She glanced down at her coat, her pulse flickering erratically. There was a bloodstain on the left side of her coat, over her heart.

Someone else's blood. She shoved the coat in the corner underneath the stairwell. Her stomach heaved.

Someone else's blood.

So there had been someone in Thomas's room with her. She *had* hurt someone. But who? Whose blood was all over her? Was it Daniel's?

Thomas moaned something she couldn't understand. With numb hands, she guided him into her lap, cradling his head in her arms.

"Careful," she said softly, as if speaking to a child. Fear surged through her as she wiped the blood from his face with her fingers, leaving a rusty stain on his cheek. This wasn't Thomas. Thomas was strong and funny and confident. The guy in her arms was scared and hurt.

"You're so beautiful, you know that?" Thomas said softly, his eyes fluttering closed. "I don't deserve a girl like you." His mouth fell open slightly and his head lolled away from her.

"Thomas?" she whispered, her voice trembling.

He didn't answer. She slipped her hand into his and watched his chest rise and fall, watched the tiny, involuntary movements of sleep. She tried not to think about the fact that she was alone. That Thomas couldn't help her. Protect her. But protect her from whom?

She wanted to believe that it wasn't Daniel, that he wasn't capable of doing such things. Not to her anyway. Yes, he could be violent. But after spending a year in a relationship with him, after everything they had shared, would he really try to physically harm her?

Suddenly she realized she had no idea. Up until this afternoon, she had thought she knew everything about him—the good and the bad. But he had lied to her about being a virgin. Had lied about one of the most important things in life. What else had he kept from her? What other secrets was he hiding? What else was he capable of?

There was only one way for her to find out whether was in Vermont. She couldn't call his cell phone this time. She had to call the resort and have him paged. If he picked up, she'd know he was there and not here. Not the one she'd slashed in the darkness of Thomas's room. Then she would know, at least, that she was safe from Daniel Ryan.

Ariana pulled her phone from her coat pocket and opened it. The screen flashed the low-battery icon, then went blank.

"No!" she groaned.

She patted Thomas's pockets, searching for his phone. Empty.

Ariana clenched her fists, feeling blood that had caked on her palms crease under her grip. What had she done to deserve this? Nothing that Daniel hadn't already done. Disgust welled up inside of her as she thought about his lies. His promises.

But Thomas was different. To him, she wasn't some girl whose mom was crazy and whose dad had to flee to another continent just to get away from it all. She was separate from her messed-up family. She was Ariana. And she *mattered* to Thomas. And for the first time in her life, that feeling mattered more than anything else. More than Billings. Maybe even more than her mother.

Drinking in the look of innocence that had settled over his features as he slept, her breath quickened. Anger poured through her, and she felt the sudden urge to scream. To hit the cement wall over and over until her knuckles bled. To make herself hurt on the outside as much as she hurt on the inside. It wasn't fair. It wasn't supposed to happen like this. To feel what she felt with Thomas only to have someone want to take it from her.

Her fingers and toes prickled with feeling as her body began to warm. She blinked, and the tears began to fall freely. Slid down her dry cheeks as she leaned against the hard cement wall, her body shaking. Cradling Thomas's still body in her arms.

Every creak of the old building, every sound that slipped through the vents and into the basement, made her cringe. Tears dripping into her lap, she closed her eyes against the darkness, but she couldn't stop the familiar feeling from creeping over her.

Ariana was totally and completely alone.

DUPLICITY

Ariana felt the light on her face before she opened her eyes. A flash-light beam swung recklessly across the basement, illuminating the tall stacks of musty boxes and the old gardening-slash-beer-pong table piled high with tools and dusty bags of fertilizer. Her heart in her throat, she sipped shaky breaths of warm, stale air as footsteps creaked above her, moving down the stairs in cautious rhythm.

Someone was coming.

She had to move Thomas in a matter of seconds. His legs were sprawled at an unnatural angle, peeking out from beneath the stairs. Carefully, she cradled his head in her hands, lowering it to the cement floor. She slipped her forearms underneath his calves, straining silently against him. His deadweight was too heavy. He didn't move an inch.

The footsteps continued down the stairs, and Ariana tugged with her last bit of strength. She wasn't ready to leave Easton. It couldn't be over for her yet. Anxious fear swept through her, and she found the strength to drag Thomas completely under the stairs and out of sight.

He mumbled something in his sleep, and the footsteps above them paused. She pressed her hand over Thomas's mouth, praying he wouldn't try to speak again. The footsteps resumed slowly, tentatively, as they navigated the darkness.

"Shit." A male voice sounded just inches from their hiding place. The bottom step cracked under the man's weight, and he stumbled into the basement. The flashlight fell to the floor and sliced across the room, spinning underneath the gardening table in the middle of the space. A sharp white light glowed parallel to the staircase, inches from Thomas's foot.

Ariana stopped breathing.

Please. Please, no, no, no.

A dark silhouette stepped into view and bent down to pick up the flashlight. Carefully, quietly, she leaned forward and peeked through the crack between the furnace and the stairwell. Residual light from the beam was just bright enough for Ariana to make out the outline of a familiar figure crouched under the table.

Mr. Holmes.

What the hell was her lit teacher doing in the Drake basement?

Warm dread trickled through Ariana's veins. It didn't matter why he was there. All that mattered was that he couldn't find her there. Of all the teachers she'd ever had at Easton, she had always respected him the most. He was smart and funny and good. And he believed the same about her. She needed him to believe the same about her.

But all that would be over if he found her on campus illegally, covered in blood, cradling the passed-out body of Easton's resident drug dealer in her arms.

Ariana bit her lip, hard. How had she ended up here? What was the matter with her? She was a Billings Girl, one of Easton's elite. This was not how she was supposed to be spending her Christmas break, hiding out like a freaking fugitive and on the verge of getting expelled.

She hated herself. Hated herself with a passion so hot it burned her skin. She wished she could strip her coat off, but Holmes was only a few feet away. And besides, she was pinned under Thomas.

The faint taste of her own blood surfaced in Ariana's mouth as she watched Mr. Holmes walk slowly to the far end of the basement, toward the windows, shining the flashlight behind boxes, underneath chairs, and over tables. He turned toward the stairwell, sweeping the light across the dirty floor. The piercing beam neared Ariana, and she ducked back under the stairs, drawing her knees up to her chest.

Had he seen her? Heard her? If he had, it was over. Mr. Holmes would have to turn them in. Her body shook with nerves as the seconds passed, feeling like hours. Any relationship she thought she'd had with Mr. Holmes would be shattered when he found out she wasn't who he thought she was. When he found out that she had lied and broken the rules.

And it wouldn't matter that she hadn't wanted to. That she wished, more than anything, that she could be the same sweet, good Ariana she'd been just a few days before. That she'd only broken the rules because it was absolutely necessary. And it was too late to turn back the clock. She screwed her eyes shut.

"You down here?" Mr. Holmes called.

Ariana's heart all but stopped. Then a delicate whisper sounded at the top of the stairs, and Mr. Holmes swung the flashlight up the stairwell.

"I'm here."

Tension flooded out of Ariana's body. Safe, at least for the moment.

"Good." His voice sounded strange in the dark. Thick.

"You wanted to see me, Mr. Holmes?" Ariana recognized the voice immediately and her pulse raced with intrigue. She heard that sweet, lilting tone laced with condescension in the halls of Billings almost every day.

Isobel Bautista.

Ariana shifted onto her knees and leaned forward, peering out from her hiding place. Risky, she knew, but she had to find out what was going on.

"I did." Mr. Holmes smirked, leaning against the gardening table and loosening his tie. "Seems I don't have a paper from you on *Madame Bovary* in my mailbox. Care to explain yourself, Miss Bautista?"

"Must have slipped my mind," she said mischievously, moving into full view. Her silky black hair tumbled down her back. She ran her fingers up his arms and across his chest, lifting her mouth to his ear. "Any way I could make it up to you?"

She pulled his tie from around his neck, tossing it on the floor. Her hands flew expertly over the buttons on his shirt, across his belt buckle as he ran his fingers through her hair. She slid onto the table and pulled him toward her. Ariana heard his breath quickening in the dark as Isobel edged off his shirt and let it fall to the floor.

Oh. My. God.

Ariana closed her eyes and sank back underneath the staircase next to Thomas. This couldn't be happening. Mr. Holmes would never have an affair with a student. He couldn't. Everyone at Easton knew that he was a good guy. A guy with a wife at home, a pregnant wife who sometimes made biscotti for him to bring to class. He wouldn't do this to her. There was no way.

Of course, the slobbering kissing sounds coming from the other side of the room suggested otherwise.

Ariana's stomach turned. She was even more disgusted with Isobel. She'd been dating her boyfriend, Jack, since freshman year. Was almost as attached to him as she was to her morning latte. Ariana had once caught her doodling the name *Mrs. John Staton* in the back of her spring issue of *Vogue*, and knew that the two of them were serious. The spring issue was Isobel's prize possession. It was common knowledge around Billings that any girl who so much as looked at her copy of the issue before Isobel read it cover to cover twice would never live to tell the tale.

And yet here they were, Mr. Holmes and Isobel, devouring each other like a pair of horny, rabid dogs in the Drake basement. Ariana felt her hands beginning to shake, and she didn't bother to stop them.

It wasn't just the fact that they were hooking up, or lying about it, or breaking all sorts of state statutory rape laws in the process. She was more pissed at herself for being so naïve as to believe that they were good people. That they were incapable of doing something so wrong. She had underestimated them, just like she'd underestimated Daniel. She'd been at Easton long enough to know that nothing was ever exactly what it seemed. Apparently, she hadn't learned the lesson well enough. She felt her hands curling tightly around Thomas's wool coat, and rage churned in the pit of her stomach.

She noticed Mr. Holmes's Dockers out of the corner of her eye. Isobel had whipped the pants toward the stairwell, and they were almost within reach. A phone peeked out of the back pocket, and Ariana glanced down at her own cell, dead on the floor next to her.

She still needed to call Daniel, to find out if he was actually in Vermont. And to do that, she needed a cell phone that actually worked. As long as Mr. Holmes was busy holding his perverted version of office hours, he wouldn't miss his cell.

Ever so carefully, Ariana inched her foot out from beneath the stairwell, keeping her gaze fixed on Mr. Holmes and Isobel to be sure they didn't see her. She nudged the pants toward her, inch by inch, until they were close enough that she could reach out and grab the cell phone without exposing herself to the happy couple.

Shielding the phone with her cupped hand, she flipped it open and stared at the screen. As her eyes adjusted to the light, the pixels on the screen coalesced to reveal a smiling pregnant woman, one hand resting on her belly. Mr. Holmes's wife was standing next to his desk, gesturing proudly with the other hand toward the nameplate that was perched on top of a stack of books. Ariana forced herself to look away from the screen. That woman deserved better than Mr. Holmes.

Don't we all deserve to be happy? Or at least to search for what we think might make us happy? Isn't that a basic human right?

Her jaw tightened as she remembered Mr. Holmes's words in class a few days ago. Now, they took on an entirely different meaning. She'd thought he was challenging the class with those words. Pushing them to go deeper. But he was just using his lecture to justify an affair with a student. And she'd been stupid enough to listen. She shook her head in disgust, cursing herself for trusting him. For always trusting the wrong people.

Her hand slipped against a button on the side of the phone, and suddenly she was staring at a crooked image of Mr. Holmes and Isobel pressed against each other. The furnace blocked part of the screen, but the flashlight on the floor offered just enough light for the screen to capture their faces.

A tiny red dot throbbed at the top of the screen next to the letters REC. The phone was recording video. Her heart started to pound in her chest. What was she doing? All she had to do to stop the recording was press the button again, but something stopped her. Ariana felt betrayed—used. Disgusted that two people whom she had admired had turned out to be so unworthy. She wanted to preserve the evidence of this moment. The evidence of their debauchery, the depth of their duplicity. Numb, she stared at the grainy image until their bodies melted out of focus on the screen.

STALKER

The sun was beginning to rise over the east edge of campus as Ariana crept toward Drake. She hadn't slept all night. Had simply stared into the darkness, her hand on Thomas's chest to monitor his breathing. In the early predawn hours, she'd slipped through one of the basement windows and sneaked back to Billings to get food. Now, she cradled in her arms the only things she'd been able to find in Noelle's closet: a bottle of SmartWater, a couple of Zone bars, and a white chocolate reindeer Dash had left on her pillow before break.

Ariana shuddered in the cold, her body feeling weak and drained. She hadn't been able to bring herself to wear the bloodstained coat she'd stashed under the basement stairwell the night before, so while she was at Billings she had grabbed her camel-colored fall jacket. It was warm, but not nearly warm enough to combat the early morning chill, its icy fingers pressing against the back of her neck and sending continuous shivers down her spine.

The sound of her boots crunching over the hardened snow cut through the crisp air. As she hurried around Drake to get to the basement, she thought she heard another sound. Footsteps moving through the snow in tandem with hers. She froze, pressing her body against the side of the building. Holding her breath, trying to quiet the sound of her throbbing heart.

Nothing but deafening silence.

Don't be stupid, Ariana. No one else is up at 5 a.m. on break. You're alone. It's all in your head.

Still, she picked up speed as she rounded the building, keeping her eyes on the ground in front of her. She couldn't bring herself to look at Ketlar. Just thinking about the deserted dorm chilled her more than the winter air. Made her feel like she was back in Thomas's room, petrified and alone. Staring at that awful photograph as a hot breath slid down her neck. Her stomach surged again at the memory. Whoever had been in there had wanted to hurt her. And had the means to do it. Worse than the idea that someone was trying to sabotage them was the suspicion that Daniel was the intruder.

Mr. Holmes's cell phone hung like a heavy weight in Ariana's pocket. She had thought about calling the resort from her room at Billings but had wanted to get back before Thomas woke up. Thinking about making the call sent her pulse into overdrive, but she had to do it. Whether he was there or—God forbid—here, she had to know. She vowed to call the moment she was safely back at Drake.

As the sun rose higher in the sky, threads of pink light played over campus, casting colorful shadows over the white snow. The beautiful sight of Easton's Gothic buildings, suddenly illuminated, should have calmed her. Ariana had always loved the way the campus looked in the early morning. The nightmares always woke her well before Noelle stirred, and she often sat at her desk to admire the view. Easton seemed so noble, so pristine in the hours before it was corrupted with students.

But instead of looking serene and untouched, the looming buildings seemed menacing, threatening.

She stopped in front of the first basement window. Something above her had moved. She looked up at the rows of windows that stretched above her. On the fourth floor, a shadow was moving in front of the window.

Startled, Ariana flung herself toward the building and pressed her back up against the wall. She checked her watch. Five fifteen a.m. Who would be up at this hour? Trying to control her breathing, she titled her head back to stare up at the window above.

The figure paused, its back to the window. In the early morning light, she recognized the dark hair. The familiar navy argyle sweater. It was Sergei. Just Sergei. Relieved, Ariana ducked down and threw the window open. She tossed everything through the opening and onto the desk she'd moved underneath the window that morning. She heard the sound of the plastic bottle rolling across the floor.

Quickly, Ariana crawled through the window, dropped down to the desk, and then to the floor. Shoulders rising and falling with her rapid breath, she chided herself for letting her curiosity get the best of her. Sergei could have seen her, not to mention any one of the other students staying behind during break. She had to be more careful.

And she had to know where Daniel was. Hands shaking, she pulled out Mr. Holmes's phone and dialed.

After one ring, a young female voice chirped in her ear. "Good morning, Winter Lodge Resort. This is Alessandra."

Ariana cleared her throat. "Yes, I'm trying to get in touch with one of your guests," she whispered into the receiver, glancing across the basement. Thomas was still sprawled out on the dusty floor, his head resting on her coat. "Daniel Ryan?"

"One moment, Miss. I'll try his room."

"Thanks," Ariana croaked.

It's fine, she told herself as the harsh ring echoed from the receiver. *It's going to be fine.*

Still, she felt sick to her stomach. If he picked up, that meant he had no idea what she'd done or whom she'd done it with. But if he picked up, he was still going to be angry. What was she going to say to him?

"Yeah?" A groggy, muffled voice sounded on the other end of the line.

Ariana gripped the phone tightly in her sweaty fist. Daniel's voice. He was in Vermont.

"Hello?" His voice sounded again, stronger this time. It was familiar, almost comforting. Ariana felt a twinge in her heart. Indecision? Remorse? But then the image of his glowing laptop screen flooded her thoughts. The image of all the names, the endless list of girls. And her name, no different from any other, at the end. She'd been a nothing to him. Just some girl that he'd counted on screwing by Christmas.

She slammed the phone shut and tossed it on the table next to her. Relief and dread filled her at once.

Daniel wasn't the one stalking her and Thomas. This was a good thing. But now she was back where she started. The person who had taken that picture had the power to ruin her life. He or she had evidence that she and Thomas had been on campus when they weren't supposed to be, that they'd been in another student's room, that they'd been doing things they definitely weren't supposed to be doing. The person who had taken that picture could destroy her. And she had no idea who that person could be.

Feeling a new wave of adrenaline rush through her, Ariana scooped up the bottle of water and the food and crouched under the stairs, next to Thomas's body.

"Thomas," she whispered. "Wake up."

She pressed her hands against his chest. His body was limp, motionless under her palms. She tried again, shaking him more violently this time.

"What the hell?" he yelled, sitting up straight. When he saw Ariana in front of him, he gripped his head with both hands and sank back onto the floor, wincing in pain. "Your wake-up calls could use a little work."

"How are you feeling?" she asked softly.

"Like somebody took a bat to my head. And my ankle."

He tested his ankle by pressing his foot into the floor and flinched, his eyes still closed.

"I'm sorry about the timing, but I need you to focus," Ariana said firmly. "I have to show you something."

She removed the folded picture of her and Thomas from her pocket. He had to see the photo—had to know what was going on.

"What is it?"

Thomas struggled to push himself up against the cement-block wall. His swiped the bottle of SmartWater and twisted the cap off, chugging half the bottle in one gulp.

Ariana dropped the picture on the floor in front of him. "I found this in your room yesterday," she began, opening Mr. Holmes's cell phone over the picture. Blue light spilled over every crease, every imperfection in the paper. "On your desk."

Looking confused, Thomas leaned over the crinkled piece of paper. Shock froze his features, and he was silent.

"Somebody's following us." Ariana was trying to sound strong, but her voice came out shaky. "And it's not Daniel. I called his resort this morning. He's there. Just like you said."

"Why?" Thomas asked, his brow creasing. "Who would—"

"I don't know," she said flatly.

She stared at the photo. Thomas was facing the camera. She was facing away. They were both sitting on Daniel's desk, amidst a pile of textbooks and dirty clothes. Daniel's laptop was open on the edge of the desk, facing the door. Once again, the thought of that spreadsheet sent a shiver of disgust through her body.

"What's that?" Thomas squinted harder at the picture, bringing it in front of his face.

"What's what?" Ariana felt her pulse quickening.

"Nothing." He shrugged. His features had hardened. "I just thought I saw something." He dropped the picture again and Ariana snatched it before it had the chance to reach the floor.

"Show me," she demanded.

The picture was the only link between them and whoever was following them. If he'd seen something that could help them figure out who it was, she needed to know.

Thomas rolled his eyes and pointed. "It's just that dark smudge in the corner of the mirror. I thought it was the photographer, but it's just ink from the printer or something." Thomas reached for the white chocolate reindeer, peeling the edge of the tinfoil away. "Never thought I'd say this, but I'm starting to wish I'd gone home for Christmas." He reached down to his ankle and touched it gingerly. "Definitely sprained."

Ariana studied the picture, trying not to let his words sting. She knew his comment hadn't meant anything, but it was hard not to take it personally.

"It's nothing," Thomas said again, biting off a giant antler. "Don't waste your time."

But Ariana's pulse was quickening again. She stood up and brought the photo over to the window, where the soft morning light was starting to gain strength. Suddenly, the smudge, as Thomas had called it, came into focus. Ariana's eyes widened in disbelief as she recognized the familiar pattern. The dark argyle plaid she'd seen just seconds ago, in the window on Drake's fourth floor.

"Oh my God." She brought her free hand to her mouth. Nervous energy rattled her insides. She should have known. How could she have been so stupid?

"What?" Thomas sat up straight.

"Sergei Tretyakov." Her voice trembled with excitement.

"The Russian kid?" he asked incredulously.

"He's *Latvian*."

"Seriously? You want to argue about this?" For the first time since they'd escaped Ketlar, Ariana saw light dancing in Thomas's eyes.

"That's his sweater, in the corner of the mirror." Ariana brought the photo over and dropped down to the floor again so that he could see it. "You were right. When he took the picture from the doorway, he accidentally got himself in the reflection."

Thomas looked skeptical. "You sure about this? I mean, why would—"

"He's always had a weird thing for me," Ariana said, intoxicated by the discovery. Now that she knew who the perpetrator was, she could do something about it. "Remember—the kid was taking so many pictures of me at the Winter Ball, Daniel had to steal his camera!" Her voice brimmed with energy. It was all starting to come together. "He's practically obsessed. So he breaks into my room and steals the picture of me. Somehow he figures out that I'm still on campus, and follows me around, leaving that photo of us in your room. It was *his* blood on my coat."

"Wait, how would he find out you're still around?" Thomas interrupted.

"I don't know," Ariana admitted. "Maybe he spotted us the other night in Hell Hall or something. He could have been there dropping off work like I was. And—oh my God. He was at North Face when I was—the hat outside the chapel must have been his!"

"Kid's a little creepy." Thomas shrugged, not looking quite convinced. "But why leave that picture for us to find? He's too lame to pull off blackmail."

"Only one way to find out," she said. "We have to break into his room."

"Oh, no," Thomas groaned. "I'm staying right here." He shrank away from her toward the wall.

She shook her head. "I can't do this alone, Thomas. And Drake is his permanent dorm. We don't even have to go outside."

Relief seeped through her heart. Sergei was a lot of things, but intimidating wasn't one of them. They could handle this. Together. She checked her watch. Two hours until breakfast.

"We'll wait until everybody leaves for breakfast and sneak in."

"I don't really have a choice, do I?" Thomas handed her the half-empty bottle of water and tore into a Zone bar.

"No. You don't," she said happily.

Ariana brought the bottle to her lips and let the cool water slide down her throat, calming her. In less than two hours, they'd have their answers.

THE MISSION

"Can you walk?" Ariana glanced worriedly at Thomas's ankle as they started up the basement stairs.

"Yeah." He grimaced at the first few steps. "Nothing I can't handle." He gripped her face in his hands, a serious look suddenly hardening his features. "Your mission, Agent Osgood, is this: Break into the Russian's room and make sure he's not hiding your picture in there." Thomas's eyes danced with amusement. "Questions?"

"Thomas," she giggled, "it's not funny. This is serious. Now come on." She held his hand as he limped slowly up the rest of the stairs.

"That's Agent Pearson to you," he retorted. "And I know it's serious. Should you accept this mission, the path through the Russian's room will be a dangerous one. There will be corduroy pants. There will be chess sets."

"Again, Latvian." Ariana rolled her ice blue eyes. "The *Latvian's* room."

"And worst of all, Agent Osgood, there will be . . ." Thomas paused dramatically, narrowing his eyes at her. "Argyle."

"I think you're still a little drugged, Agent Pearson," Ariana said with a laugh.

"Nothing wrong with that," Thomas said.

Ariana paused and leaned back against the stairwell, wanting to enjoy the lightness of the moment. After everything they had been through in the past two days, laughing with Thomas felt good. It felt normal. And, glancing out the windows, she noticed for the first time that morning how beautiful the campus looked underneath the thick covering of snow. It was as if someone had taken a white cashmere throw and tossed it casually over the grounds. The trees, the old stone buildings, the lampposts—everything was draped in pure white. Under the bright sunlight, Easton Academy looked innocent. Untouched.

"You ready?" she said finally, her hand on the door handle.

"Yep." Thomas nodded, glancing suspiciously around the deserted basement. "Let's move, Osgood."

"You are such a dork," she groaned. "When the guys get back to campus I'm going to tell all of them what a dork you are," she lied. She wasn't exactly sure which parts of this weekend she would ever divulge, but she was just having fun—and trying to keep her mind from wondering if the stalker really was Sergei and if he was actually dangerous.

Together they slipped into the darkened lobby of Drake House. Ariana lifted her index finger to her lips, motioning for Thomas to be quiet. He gave her an exaggerated nod and she had to concentrate to stifle a giggle while he checked the directory board to find Sergei's room number.

"He's on four," Thomas said as he limped to the elevator.

In moments, Ariana found herself staring at a dorm door covered in photographs. Shots of the Easton Academy campus. Pictures of buildings, professors, and students. There was a shot of Noelle giving the camera the finger at the Winter Ball, a look of annoyance tinged with self-satisfaction on her face. A candid of Dash and Thomas, tossing a football across the quad. A picture of the entire student body, taken from the back of the Easton chapel during the last morning assembly. Brilliant red and blue light filtered through the stained glass and spilled over the students. It was a stunning image. All the images were, in their own way. Somehow, Sergei had managed to capture something about Easton that Ariana couldn't name. What Easton was, who its students were, when no one was looking, when it was stripped of the polished veneer of money, prestige, and power. Sergei had captured what was underneath.

"There you are." Thomas pointed.

Ariana's breath caught in her throat. In the photo, she was leaning against the marble column at the Driscoll, staring up at the ceiling, the light from the crystal chandelier spilling over her face and hair. She couldn't take her eyes away from the girl in that picture. There was an innocence about her that seemed foreign. That girl felt safe and secure in the world. She trusted that everything was going to work out for her in the end. Ariana felt an unexpected twinge of anger.

"Ariana?" Thomas rested his hand on her shoulder and she flinched.

"What?" she snapped. Her voice severed the space between them like a razor blade.

Thomas looked surprised. "Nothing. I just thought you wanted to get this over with."

Ariana avoided his gaze. "You're right. Let's go." She pushed Sergei's door open and tried the light switch on the wall. It worked. "Power's back on."

Sergei's room was sparse and perfectly organized. His books and notebooks were stacked in symmetrical piles on his desk, and his bed was made so tightly, Ariana wondered whether he had ever actually slept in it. The attention to detail was familiar—comforting, in a weird way. It was a lot like Ariana's room.

A single photograph of an older-looking man and woman hung above his dresser. And sitting on his nightstand, next to a tiny travel alarm clock, was another photograph. A black-and-white photograph of Ariana, blowing a kiss to the camera.

"Found it." She sank onto the edge of Sergei's bed in disbelief, staring into her own eyes. No matter how sure she'd sounded earlier, part of her still hadn't believed Sergei could do such a thing. He was so unassuming, so quiet. But who knew what churned beneath his calm exterior? For the first time since she'd spotted the telltale argyle in the picture of her and Thomas, she felt afraid.

Thomas collapsed onto the bed next to her. "Got the camera," he said, holding up Sergei's Nikon. "Your boyfriend must have given it back before he left." He held it up so Ariana could see and pressed the display button at slow intervals. "But he let the Latvian keep his photos."

Ariana stared at the glowing images on the display screen. Snapshots of her walking to class, clutching her books tightly to her chest. A picture of her and Noelle, laughing in the cafeteria. Countless images of her sitting alone, reading. And shot after shot of her at the Winter Ball. Nuzzling Daniel's neck. Taking a sip of champagne. Twirling a lock of hair around her index finger.

She leaned against Thomas, suddenly feeling weak. "I had no idea he was this . . ." She couldn't even finish her sentence. There must have been dozens of images of her in Sergei's camera. Scrolling through them was like watching a slide show of her life for the past few months. Everything she'd done, everywhere she'd been, was right at her fingertips.

"Oh my God," Ariana gasped.

The screen had just landed on a picture of her and Thomas as they entered the old chapel in the woods the other night, followed by a photo of Eli heading back in the direction of town. He'd probably caught the last train to Greenwich that night. Smart guy.

"I was right. He's been following us this whole time," she said, shoving the camera at Thomas. "What is *wrong* with him?"

She pushed away from the bed, clutching the framed picture in her hand. The familiar feeling of panic clawed at her once again, threatening to drag her under. If Sergei was capable of stalking her like this, what else could he do to her?

"Thomas, what if he *is* planning on blackmailing us?" Ariana said shakily. "He has dozens of pictures of us from the last two days. He could get us expelled in a heartbeat."

"Ariana, it's okay." Thomas's voice sounded far away. A loud beep emanated from the camera. "I just deleted all the files."

"But he could have saved them on his computer. Or worse, an Internet account. That's not a guarantee that—"

Thomas put the camera down and placed both hands on her shoulders. "It's okay. We'll take care of it."

Ariana stared into Thomas's eyes, but she barely heard him. Sergei could ruin everything. If she got expelled, her life would be over. She would never graduate from Easton, never get into Princeton, never have the life she and her mother had planned for her.

And she would never see Thomas again. She couldn't let that happen. For the first time in her life, she was actually *living*. She was herself when she was with Thomas. Ariana, and nobody else. She couldn't go back to the way things were before. Couldn't go back to pretending. It would kill her.

Thomas was right. They were going to take care of this. Starting now.

Heart thundering, Ariana whirled around to the door and froze.

Sergei was standing in the doorway, his cold gaze fixed on her.

SO EASY

"You son of a bitch," Thomas hissed, grimacing as he tried to put weight on his bad ankle.

There was something in Sergei's dark eyes that sent tiny, electric chills through Ariana's body. She recognized it instantly; the look that had surfaced in her mother's eyes years ago and had never left. Desperation.

Sergei glanced from Thomas to Ariana to the photo in her hand, to the camera on his desk, and back again. Instantly, the desperation in his eyes morphed into fear. He turned from the doorway and ran.

"Sergei! Wait!" Ariana shouted, dropping the picture of herself on the bed and bolting for the door. She sprinted down the hallway behind Sergei. "We just want to talk to you!"

With every step, the gap between them widened. Ariana had never been much of an athlete, but she couldn't let him get away.

"Kid's fast," Thomas huffed from behind her. His voice crackled with pain.

Ariana didn't take the time to answer. She reached the stairwell and flew down the steps three at a time, slamming into the door at the foot of the stairs just as Sergei slammed it shut behind him. She smashed her fist against the heavy wood.

"Damnit!" She doubled over, gasping for breath.

"You okay?" Thomas was moving slowly down the steps one floor above. She looked up at him, feeling a sudden pang of guilt. She shouldn't leave him alone in his condition.

"He's getting away," Ariana said desperately.

"Just go!" Thomas shouted, his voice bouncing down the stairwell. "I'll catch up!"

Without another glance in his direction, Ariana threw open the back door and squinted against the glare of the sun's reflection on the snow. Sergei had crossed the stretch of land behind Drake House and was headed into the woods. She gritted her teeth and followed with renewed determination. She *would* get to him. If he revealed those photos—the photos that showed her *cheating* on Daniel—she would lose everything. It wouldn't matter that Daniel had lied or that he'd cheated first. All that would matter was that she cheated on Paige's twin brother. She'd lose her friends, Billings, maybe even her mother. She would be a nothing.

Sergei disappeared into the thick covering of trees ahead. Every nerve in her body seized with terror. Reaching the edge of the woods, Ariana turned back for a moment to look for Thomas. He was limping slowly toward her, at least twenty-five yards behind. She inhaled a sharp breath and ducked past the line of trees into the woods.

The crunch of leaves and branches under Sergei's feet slowed up ahead. He was getting winded and she was getting closer. She weaved through clusters of old pine trees and ducked underneath their heavy boughs, adrenaline propelling her forward. Sergei was just ahead, struggling against a branch thick with pine needles. He shoved past it and it whipped back in her direction, the tip of the branch slicing across her face.

She brought her hand to her numb cheek. When she pulled it away, her fingers were covered in blood. Stinging anger rose inside her. Why was he torturing her like this? Sergei had her whole life in his hands. Easton, Billings, her mother, and Thomas.

"Sergei!" she screamed, tears running down her cheeks "Stop! Please!" Her desperation was palpable, and it rose up in her throat, threatening to choke her. He hurried into the large clearing at the center of the woods. The lake stretched in front of them, silent and frozen.

Ariana had spent so much time around this lake since she'd come to Easton as a freshman. Bonfires with the other Billings Girls in the fall, stretching out on blankets with a bottle of white wine in the spring. The threat of getting caught had always sent a shiver of excitement down her spine, a kind of excitement she'd never felt when she'd lived at home. The threat she faced now filled her with gut-wrenching dread.

Sergei darted onto the frozen surface, then hesitated, glancing over his shoulder at her. She ran faster, the space between them diminishing with every step. Reaching toward him, she strained to grab the hem of his sweater. She was so close.

Suddenly, he stopped and turned around to face her. Before she realized what he had done, her body slammed into his. They tumbled onto the ice together. Her head cracked against the unforgiving surface, and she felt a searing pain at the base of her skull. The sounds of their heaving gasps throbbed in her ears.

And then another sound, this one sharp. Slow at first, then faster. The crackling sound of ice breaking underneath their weight.

Ariana screamed, flipping onto her stomach in time to see the ice give way under Sergei's body.

"Oh my God," Ariana gasped.

A look of surprise flashed across Sergei's sweaty face right before he plunged into the gray water. Ariana instinctively slid backward, away from the hole that threatened to swallow them both, but Sergei's fingers closed around her ankle.

"No! Let go of me!" Ariana screamed, clawing at the ice beneath her, leaving a jagged trail in the ice as Sergei pulled her closer and closer.

"Help!" Sergei croaked. "Help me!"

His grip was like a vice. She could see the freezing water getting closer as he thrashed with his free arm. In seconds he was going to pull her down with him. They were both going to die.

"Sergei, no!" Ariana choked. Fear honed her senses, and suddenly everything around her came into sharp focus. She reached down to her ankle and grabbed his hand, her fingers digging into his ashen skin. His face twisted in fear and pain.

"Please," he gasped, thrashing in the water. "Help me! I don't swim!"

His voice echoed in the silent clearing. The color was slipping rapidly from his cheeks. He couldn't survive for more than a few minutes in the icy lake, and she wasn't sure that she was strong enough to pull him to safety. She grabbed his forearm with her other hand and pulled as hard as she could.

"Hold on," she groaned, leaning back with all her weight. She couldn't silence the sound of her heart pounding in her chest. The sound of Sergei, screaming for help. The warmth in her mother's voice that surfaced every time she mentioned Daniel. Thomas's breath on her skin, the soft sound of him whispering her name while they lay in bed. The voices echoed in her mind, getting louder and louder. Closing in. Suffocating her.

You never know what people are capable of until they're pushed to their edge, Ariana.

"Ariana!" Sergei begged.

"Shut up!" she screamed. The images he'd taken of her and Thomas flashed in mind. It was all too much. Too chaotic. She needed silence, time to think. Sergei's grip loosened slightly, and she looked down at him. A bluish-gray tint had crept into his skin. He mumbled something about his photographs, looking up at her with wide, pleading eyes. A gnawing sensation at the back of her mind told her that it wasn't too late to help him. To save him.

But those pictures. Why had he taken them? What did he want for his silence? What would he make her do to keep quiet? Her life was on the line here. He'd backed her into a corner.

"Please." Sergei's voice was a whimper now.

She locked eyes with him. And suddenly everything became clear.

Slowly, deliberately, Ariana released her grip on his arm. Sergei's eyes went wide as she placed her hand on his dark, wet head, and pushed. Pushed with all her strength. He struggled for a moment. Just for a moment. But he was weak. And before long he slipped silently underneath the ice. His eyes dark, unblinking, stared up at her from under the glassy gray surface. And then he was gone. Vanished. As if he had never existed.

A thin film of new ice was forming over the hole he'd fallen through. She stared at her reflection in the icy water, sinking into the silence that hung heavy over the clearing. A strange warmth settled over her as she sat on the ice.

It had been so easy. She had taken control back. She'd get to keep Billings, her mother, Thomas. She'd have time to figure it all out perfectly. And with that thought, her mind was finally calm. Free. The voices had quieted.

All but one.

"Ariana!" Thomas's voice boomed across the lake, and she glanced up to see him limping toward her. "What happened? Where's Sergei?"

"Stay there!" she yelled. "The ice isn't thick enough!"

Thomas froze, and she pushed herself slowly across the ice, careful to stay low. When she reached him at the edge of the lake, she wrapped her arms around his legs, squeezing them tight. He was here. And they were safe.

EVERYTHING

"We have to get out of here. Now," Ariana rasped, grabbing Thomas and pulling him back toward campus. Away from the lake. Away from Sergei's body.

"Ariana." He grabbed her arm, refused to let her run. "You have to tell me what happened out there."

She searched his face. Took in his furrowed brow, the way his mouth twitched slightly. He could never know the truth. He wouldn't understand.

"He grabbed me. He . . . he tried to hit me," she said. There was a waver in her voice. Good. It sounded like she was scared, trembling. Really, she was waiting. Waiting for the gravity of what had just happened to weigh her down, drag her under. Waiting for the guilt to suffocate her. Just waiting for the calm to break. Waiting to feel.

But all she felt was . . . peace. *It had been so easy.* All her problems gone—just like that.

"He tried to hit you?" Thomas repeated.

"I managed to shove him off of me, but when he hit the ice it broke underneath him." Her voice was steady and calm, and the explanation slipped from her lips with little effort. "He fell in and I tried to save him, but I wasn't strong enough."

For a brief moment, she thought she saw uncertainty in Thomas's eyes, felt him shrink away. But then he was holding her, pulling her close.

"Your face," he whispered when he pulled away. He reached out and touched her cheek where the pine branch had sliced her skin. "Is that where he—"

Ariana nodded. She pulled in a choppy breath, pleased by how broken she sounded despite her Zen-like peace.

"We have to tell the police," Thomas said.

Ariana pulled away. "No!"

"What? Why not? Ariana, someone died. We're the only people that know what happened," Thomas said. He folded his shaking hands over his chest. "We have to do something."

"Thomas, please." Ariana forced herself to sound weak, vulnerable. "If we call the police, we'll have to explain everything. We'll be expelled. Maybe arrested. And my mother, your parents . . . what about your third strike?"

Thomas's blue eyes hardened and Ariana knew she'd hit home. Thomas's survival instinct had kicked in. He needed to protect himself—and her. She was just as important to him as he was to her. She knew it was true.

"Shit. Okay. Okay. You're right." Thomas pushed his hand through his hair, his eyes rimmed in red. "Okay. We have to get out of here." He gripped her hand tight. "I can't fucking believe this."

His face twisted in pain as he leaned on his bad ankle and they started the trek back. Ariana relished the feel of his warm hand over hers as they made their way through the trees. Everything was fine. She was with Thomas and everything was going to be fine. It was romantic, even, this early morning walk through the woods. So serene, so peaceful. They should do this every morning once school was back in session. . . .

"We have to leave campus," Thomas said softly. "Separate for a while."

"What?"

Ariana was floored by the suggestion, by the sudden break in her happy thoughts. Her body tensed with anger and she stopped abruptly. How could he be so quick to leave her, after everything they'd been through together? After what she had just done for them? For him? He couldn't just leave her alone.

"No." Her voice was like ice. "We can't. I won't do it," she said as she stared through him.

"We have to." Thomas started to take a step toward her, but something stopped him. He looked at her uncertainly. Was that fear in his eyes? What did he have to be afraid of? "We don't have a choice, Ariana. They're going to figure out Sergei's missing and question everyone who was on campus. If they find out we were here, we're more than screwed."

"I know that," she snapped. "But I'm not going to leave you now, Thomas. Not when we just found each other," she said more calmly.

Thomas snorted a laugh. "Just found each other? What is this, some kind of cheesy soap opera?"

Ariana's eyes smoldered with anger. She clutched her arm, digging into her jacket sleeve with her fingernails. "Don't mock me," she said tersely.

Thomas blinked. "I'm not."

"Yes, you are!" Ariana shouted, startling a crow out of its perch in a nearby tree—sending it squawking toward the sky.

She stared into his eyes and waited, her teeth clenched. He loved her. She knew he did. He had to love her. Because if he didn't . . .

Thomas gazed back at her for a long moment. Looked at her as if he was seeing her for the first time. Finally, he stepped forward and took her hand. "I don't want to be away from you either. But Ariana, please. Be reasonable. If I get caught, I'll lose everything. My family, my friends, my inheritance . . ." He looked deep into her eyes and touched her face with his cold hand. "I'll lose *you*."

Ariana's heart surged. He did love her. She knew it. She slipped her arms under his and held him tight.

"Okay," she whispered, gripping him tighter with each passing second. His body shook against hers. "Whatever you want to do. We'll be fine." She lifted her face to his and kissed him. "Trust me. No one will ever know."

"Okay." Thomas exhaled a shaky breath. His eyes were glassy. "Now let's get out of here."

He slung his arm over her shoulder and, leaning into each other, they limped toward campus. Ariana breathed evenly, deliberately, letting the cold, fresh air cleanse her. With every step, she left Sergei farther behind. Every moment that passed would put more distance between them, until he was nothing but a vague memory, a kid who might have gone to Easton Academy once. A fading image in an old, yellowed photograph.

HARDEST THING

An hour later they stood together at the corner of the main inter-
section in downtown Easton. The streets were blanketed in darkness,
save for the tiny orbs of light from the streetlamps on every corner.
Ariana leaned against the cold iron base of one of the lampposts,
staring numbly past Thomas to the other side of the street. The bou-
tiques had closed hours ago. Mannequins frozen in unnatural poses
gaped at her from the other side of darkened windows. She shivered
as a sharp wind whipped around the corner, carrying gusts of pow-
dered snow with it.

"Say something," Thomas pleaded, kicking at the dirty ice that had
accumulated along the edge of the brick-lined sidewalk. He stuffed
his hands in his jacket pockets, peering worriedly at her from under
his wool hat.

"What do you want me to say?" Ariana couldn't bring herself to
look at him. Did he want her to say that she wasn't ready for this? That

she wanted just one more night with him before she had to leave? That the thought of going to Vermont to be with Daniel made her chest feel so tight she thought she might explode? She'd said all of those things. But she was still standing at the corner, her bag slung over her shoulder, the minutes they had left together slipping past her like the wind. She had to remind herself that what they had planned was worth it.

They had talked everything through as they'd made the trek downtown. Trains were running again because it had finally stopped snowing, and already several inches had melted off. Even though she hated the cold, Ariana would have stayed snowed in forever if it meant being with Thomas. But they had to stick to the plan. If Ariana were to break up with Daniel now and start seeing Thomas, it would raise suspicions. Especially in Paige, who would undoubtedly spend most of break grilling Ariana about exactly where she'd been and what she'd done. So Thomas had decided—well, *they* had decided together, really—to let all this mess with Sergei die down. They could still sneak around this year, but she'd have to wait until the summer to break up with Daniel. Then she and Thomas could be together in September. Daniel and Paige would be gone, and they could just start dating, like it was brand-new. They would spend their senior year together, as a real couple. Just her and Thomas.

"I don't know what I want you to say. Anything, I guess." Thomas reached out to touch her face, and she started as his fingertips grazed her cheek. Her skin felt raw. The cold was like sandpaper, scraping away her protective layers. Leaving her exposed.

Silently, Ariana wrapped her thin camel coat tight around her frame to block the wind, but it didn't help. She thought longingly of her white winter coat, now a pile of ashes in the clearing on the hill. She had gone back there, to the place where she and her friends had partied on so many warm autumn nights, and burned all the evidence of her two days on campus. The first thing she would do in Vermont was buy a new winter coat.

Thomas moved closer to her, resting his ungloved hands on her shoulders. Cupping her neck, her jaw, with his hands.

"Look at me," he ordered. She did as she was told. Looked him right in the eye. "I don't want to do this either. You know that, right?"

"I know." She nodded, letting him pull her close. She knew he was right, knew this was the only way. And she wasn't making this any easier for him.

"You remember what you're going to tell them?" he asked gently.

"That I got caught in a motel on the border of Connecticut for two nights because of the snow," she repeated robotically.

"Good." He gave her a rare, sincere smile. "It's only two weeks, naughty girl. We can do two weeks, right?"

He nudged her foot with his. The sound of that nickname, that stupid nickname, brought tears to her eyes. She wiped them away with the back of her hand. Two weeks in Vermont sounded like an eternity. But it was the only way she'd have an alibi. People to vouch for where she'd been over break. Even if those people had to be Daniel and Paige Ryan.

"Don't call me naughty girl," she joked lamely.

"Please. You love it." Thomas grinned. But his eyes were blank.

Dead. And for the first time, she saw that he was just as miserable as she was. "I want you to have something." He reached into his pocket. It was the old New York City subway token he'd been fiddling with at the Winter Ball. He pressed it into her hand. "I've carried this around forever. It's lucky. It'll be our thing, our symbol or whatever."

The sound of sirens punctured the night air, and Ariana froze as two police cruisers sped down the street toward them in a blur. Red and blue light slipped across Thomas's face, then disappeared.

"You don't think—" Ariana began, her voice shaking.

"Hey. You have to keep it together, okay?" He pulled her closer, lowering his mouth to her ear. "They won't find him," he said softly. "And even if they do, they won't think to ask either one of us about it. I was on my way to New York, and you were on your way to Vermont."

"On my way to Vermont," she echoed. As if repeating the words would make them true.

"To Daniel," Thomas said somberly.

A fresh wave of tears sprang to her eyes. She knew what he meant. Daniel was going to expect her to have sex with him. Could she actually go to Vermont and do that? Could she sleep with Daniel, tell him she loved him, when all she wanted to do was be with Thomas? The thought of lying in bed next to Daniel made her stomach lurch.

Ariana pressed her cheek against Thomas's warm wool jacket and leaned into him. In that moment all she wanted was to be with him. To leave Easton and Billings, Daniel and her mother, behind. Start over. Just her and Thomas. No one else.

"Hey," she murmured into his chest, "want to come with me? I hear there's this really *exclusive* resort there."

"I wish." Thomas kissed the top of her head and held her face in his hands. "Just remember that you're not just some name on a list, Ariana. You're better than that. You deserve better than that."

A white taxi with a green-checkered border turned the corner and slowed at the curb and suddenly, Ariana couldn't breathe. It was as if the air had been sucked out of her lungs, leaving her deflated.

Thomas kissed her. Hard. Frantic, she tried to memorize everything about him. The lines of his body under her fingertips, and the softness of his lips. The way that lock of hair fell into his face and brushed against her forehead. She didn't want to lose any of it.

He pulled away and kissed her lightly on the nose. "You gonna be okay?"

She nodded slowly.

"See you in two weeks," he said, pulling open the door of the cab.

"Two weeks."

Somehow, Ariana made herself pull away from him, even though the pain in her heart was excruciating. She slipped into the backseat, and the slam of the cab door made her jump. Thomas stood on the sidewalk, gazing down at her through the foggy window. Ariana grasped at the memory of his kiss.

The cab lurched, forcing her to face forward. When she turned around again, Thomas was gone.

"Where you headed?" the cabbie asked gruffly from the front seat.

"Train station," she replied flatly.

A Christmas tree—shaped air freshener swung from the rearview mirror, filling the cab with the thick stench of pine. Traces of cigarette smoke and sweat seemed to rise up from the torn leather seats. Breathing through her mouth to block the stench, Ariana pulled Mr. Holmes's cell phone from her coat pocket. She blocked the number before dialing.

"Hello?" Daniel answered after the first ring.

"It's me." Ariana kept her voice low.

"Who is this? Wait a minute. You sound familiar. A little like my girlfriend." Ariana couldn't decide whether Daniel sounded relieved or angry. She decided she didn't have the energy to care.

"It was the storm. I couldn't get out," she replied, her words clipped.

"My parents keep asking about you. Asking when you're coming. Don't really know what to tell them, Ariana."

Annoyed. Definitely annoyed.

"I'll be there tonight." Already she felt tired.

"Tonight?" The edge in Daniel's voice suddenly softened. "I'll meet you at the station. What time does your train get in?"

She heard rustling papers over the familiar sound of ESPN in the background.

"I don't know yet," she said quickly. "Don't bother coming to the station. It'll be late. I'll meet you at the lodge, okay?"

She screwed her eyes shut, praying that Daniel would agree. She needed time. Time to transform herself into the sweet, smiling girlfriend she'd have to play for the next two weeks. The more time she had, the better.

"You sure?" Daniel sounded uncertain.

"Yeah. I'll call you when I get to the lobby."

"Okay. So I'll see you when you get here," Daniel paused, and silence buzzed over the line. "I love you, Ariana."

She felt every muscle in her body tighten. "Me too," she managed.

Without another word, she flipped the phone closed and shoved it in her pocket. Her fingers hit the subway token. She smiled and took off her necklace, placing the token next to the fleur-de-lis, and refastened the chain around her neck.

WORTH IT
JANUARY OF JUNIOR YEAR

It was late Sunday afternoon when Daniel and Ariana's cab pulled through Easton's gates. Most of the snow had melted over the rest of break. Ariana's heart jumped with excitement as the cabdriver navigated his way expertly around the front circle, avoiding pockets of students dragging designer suitcases in their wake.

She turned toward the window and shook her head at the sight of London Simmons and Vienna Clark, the sophomores whose copy-and-paste style had quickly earned them the nickname the Twin Cities. The girls struggled with hot pink Chanel suitcases, their faces scarlet with effort. Or second-degree burns, judging from their identical sunglass tans and the bottle of duty-free rum peeking out of Vienna's Halston beach tote.

"What's that smile for?" Daniel slipped his arm around her shoulders. It felt heavy, like it was filled with lead.

Ariana shrugged, itching to be away from his touch but forcing herself to grin at him. "Just glad to be back."

Daniel groaned, reaching into his back pocket for his wallet as the cab slowed to a stop.

"Not me. Two weeks went by way too fast."

He fished a fifty out of his wallet and handed it to the driver, then jumped out and hurried around to the other side to open Ariana's door.

"Thank you," Ariana said sweetly, stepping onto the curb.

The crisp winter air sent a shiver of anticipation down her spine. Every day for two weeks, she'd fantasized about this moment. Getting back to Easton. Getting back to Thomas. She glanced down at her watch, adjusting it against the glare of the late afternoon sun.

"Want to go into town for dinner?" Daniel was standing idly by as the cabdriver lugged each of their bags from the trunk and tossed them on the curb. "I'm starving."

"No," she said, too quickly. Realizing her mistake, she forced a yawn. "I'm just really exhausted."

She tugged anxiously at the puke green cashmere scarf Daniel's mom had given her for Christmas. She'd felt obligated to wear it during the entire trip, and now it felt like it was tightening around her throat.

Daniel frowned. "Okay. Then lunch tomorrow?" Effortlessly, he picked up a duffel bag bulging with ski equipment and slung it over one shoulder.

"Sure. Sounds fun," Ariana conceded, her heart sinking. She picked up her bag, stealing another glance at her watch as they headed toward Billings.

"Got someplace to be?" Daniel smirked. She hated when he looked at her like that. Like she was a child he kept around for his amuse-ment.

"Almost past my bedtime," she joked, forcing a laugh. An overwhelm-ing sense of relief surfaced as she saw Billings looming ahead. Her escape. "So I'll see you tomorrow?" she said hastily, her steps quickening.

Daniel nodded, and she watched him disappear in the crowds of students swarming around the dorms.

Ariana waited for a few agonizing minutes before running up the front steps of Billings. Throwing open the front door, she tossed her bag in the entryway, then sprinted back down the steps and through the maze of dorms, tuning out the idle holiday gossip that buzzed around her. As she passed Drake and neared Ketlar, she scanned the pockets of students around her, searching for any sign of Daniel. Good. He was nowhere to be found.

Gwendolyn Hall stretched just beyond the line of trees at the edge of campus. Easton's oldest building had been deserted years ago, and Ariana had never had reason to venture inside. She stared up at the infamous façade. The frozen, overgrown weeds and brush beneath the boarded-up windows seemed to be reaching up like wiry fin-gers, threatening to strangle the old landmark. Two crumbling stone benches flanked the entrance, hidden by overgrown trees and shrubs. Cautiously, she lowered herself onto the closest bench, checking her watch again. The only sound she heard was that of her own foot tapping against the cracked cement walkway.

"Could've warned me you were planning on showing up fashion-ably late."

Ariana heard his voice before she saw him. She leaped to her feet, looking around her.

Finally, Thomas emerged from the side of the building. His hair was shorter on the sides and he looked older, somehow. Broader. Even more perfect.

She almost tripped over a jagged piece of cement on the ground as she ran toward him. When she threw himself into his arms, he staggered under her momentum.

"Easy!" He laughed, kissing her face, her hair.

"You have no idea how much I missed you," Ariana breathed.

"Come on. Only door that isn't boarded up leads to the basement."

He tugged her hand and led her around the side of the building, through the dead brush that lined the walls. Thomas gripped the door handle and yanked it open, ducking through the doorway. She followed him into the deserted basement. Musty, damp air hung thick around them. She unwound the ugly scarf from around her neck and slipped out of her new, light blue Dior coat. It took about two seconds for her to give up on finding a clean place to lay them, and she tossed them over a dusty chair in the corner. That was what dry cleaners were for.

"I felt like I was going crazy." Ariana pulled the wooden door closed behind them. Slivers of dusty light from the setting sun filtered through its cracks, painting red slashes across their bodies.

"Me too." Thomas pinned her to the stone wall, tugging her sweater over her head. He ran his fingers through her hair; kissed her on the mouth, the neck, along her collarbone. She hadn't felt like this the whole time she'd been in Vermont. She had missed feeling the way she did when she was with Thomas. Missed feeling alive, free. "At least you didn't have to spend two weeks holed up in your parents' co-op with your moron of a brother."

"Awwww. Poor thing," she said with a laugh. "Life on the Upper East Side must be *so* hard."

He shrugged out of his coat and yanked his sweater off over his head. "Like you were roughing it in Vermont," he said, his hands traveling over her skin.

Her body tensed under his touch. The last person she wanted to think about when she was with Thomas was Daniel. She wanted to forget about the last two weeks with the Ryans, let the memory of everything that had happened between Daniel and her evaporate, like her breath in the winter air.

"What's wrong?" Thomas breathed into her ear. He pressed his hands against her hips, guiding her through the maze of student desks piled high around the basement. Her legs backed into an old oak desk shoved against the far wall, and he lifted her onto it. "You okay?"

"Of course," she said quickly, slipping her arms around him and pulling him close. "I'm fine."

Suddenly, a familiar buzzing sound escaped from her back pocket.

"My phone," she gasped.

"Ignore it."

"I can't." She yanked the phone out and her heart sank. Paige Ryan was calling her. She pressed her palms against his chest and pushed him gently away. "I have to get back."

"Oh." Realization slipped over Thomas's face. "Got a hot date?" He backed off quickly, grabbing his sweater off the floor.

"No, it's just Paige," she said. "She's going to start wondering where I am, and she already asked soooo many questions over break about what I did by myself in a motel for two days and—"

"It's fine," he said, leaning in to kiss her lightly on the lips.

"I know this sneaking around sucks, but it's kind of exciting, too," she said suggestively, looking up at him through her thick lashes.

"Sure," Thomas said as he got dressed.

Adrenaline still pulsed through Ariana, and every cell in her body screamed for her to stay with Thomas. To forget about Daniel.

"It's all going to be worth it," she said, reaching for his belt loop and pulling him to her. "We just have to wait it out until the fall, and then we can be together, right?"

"Right," Thomas replied with another quick kiss.

"And in the meantime, we can keep meeting up here," she said coyly. "Like tomorrow? Around five? Maybe we can finish what we just started."

She pulled him closer to her and bit his bottom lip playfully. Thomas grinned.

"Promise?"

"Promise."

She kissed him deeply, digging her nails into his hair and holding him tightly until she finally broke away. Smiling, Ariana picked up her sweater and coat and quickly redressed.

"If there's one thing you should know about me, Thomas Pearson, it's that I don't like unfinished business," she said, dusting the dirt off her coat. "I always see everything through to the very end."

"Good to know," Thomas said groggily.

She tugged on the front of his coat and pulled him in for a final kiss. "See you later."

Ariana stepped outside and took a deep breath. She hated leaving Thomas, but they both knew that she had to go. Paige couldn't start asking questions again.

Trudging around the side of Gwendolyn Hall, Ariana ducked under low tree branches and stepped through brown grass matted with snow. Gray clouds had started to shift slowly over campus, casting smoky shadows over the looming buildings that dotted the grounds. In the eerie afternoon light, Easton Academy looked deserted. Ariana braced herself against a sudden gust of wind, trying to ignore the feeling of dread that began to weigh on her as she headed back toward Billings. She hadn't even thought about what she'd say when she saw Noelle. Noelle, who could read her with a single glance.

Ariana steeled herself and headed into the wind. The next few months were going to be one big act. It wouldn't be easy, she knew, but her hard work would pay off in September. In September, when she and Thomas would finally be together for real. Forever.

NO GOOD REASON

Ariana shifted uncomfortably in the vinyl booth, staring at the laminated menu in front of her. She had agreed to meet Daniel for lunch after her morning class. Predictably, he'd chosen 24/7, an overcrowded diner that served greasy burgers and fries to Easton Academy students twenty-four hours a day. In all the time that she and Daniel had been together, they'd never tried another restaurant for lunch. Never mind the fact that the only vegetarian dishes on the menu were the fries and a weak attempt at a side salad. He had never once asked if she wanted to try something different. And she had never complained.

"Order up!" a cook yelled from behind the counter, startling her. She checked her watch. Daniel was ten minutes late. She'd give him five more minutes before she headed back to campus. They had been back for less than a day, and already he was keeping her waiting.

"Hey, babe." Daniel appeared next to her, leaning down to give her a quick peck. His lips were rough against her cheek. "Sorry I'm late. Coach wanted to see me after class." He slid into the booth across from her and rested his hands on top of hers, giving them a squeeze. "Been here long?" His cheeks were flushed from the cold.

Ariana shook her head, trying to shake the disappointment she felt at the very sight of him.

"I was running late too," she said with a small smile.

She lifted her hand to her chest, touching the subway token that hung on the chain beneath her cashmere turtleneck, and searched Daniel's face for any sign that he knew. Nothing.

"Good." He pulled a menu from behind the silver napkin dispenser and opened it on the table. "God, it feels good in here. It's freezing out there," he said, rubbing his hands together and blowing into them. "Did you hear about your little friend Sergei?"

Ariana's heart all but stopped. Daniel glanced up at her.

"They found his body in the lake. Idiot went up there by himself and apparently drowned." Daniel sounded amused.

"That's awful," Ariana said, forcing her features into a look of surprised horror even as relief flooded her body. An accidental drowning.

Perfect.

Daniel's brow knit. Suddenly he was all serious. "I know. But it makes you think, doesn't it? Could have been one of us. We're up there all the time. Someone could stagger out there drunk and *bam!*"

Ariana jumped in her seat.

"The ice breaks and that's it. Over," he said, shaking his head as he looked at the menu.

"Well, maybe we should start hanging out somewhere else," Ariana suggested, her mouth dry.

"Yeah. Maybe."

Ariana's skin felt tight. She closed her eyes against the garish light that poured over them from the swinging lamps overhead. She hated everything about being in this place with him: the sound of screaming children and cooks yelling out orders, the dizzying black-and-white checkered floor, the smell of grease hanging thick in the stale air. She took a slow, deep breath.

Why did she have to do this? No one gave a crap about Sergei. Daniel had just made that perfectly clear. So why, why, why was she here?

Ariana clutched her arm and breathed in and out.

Keep it together. This is all for Thomas. I have to stick to the plan. There's too much at risk.

"Anyhow, Coach told me he got a call from the head coach at Harvard the other day," Daniel said. "They want me to play there in the fall. The guy said he was really impressed with what he saw when he came down for homecoming." He closed his menu and slid it to the edge of the table.

"That's great," she said brightly, resting her forearms on the table between them and leaning toward him. "I'm really proud of you." The words spilled from her mouth effortlessly, as if they'd been scripted.

"Only problem is, my dad doesn't want me to play during my first semester." Daniel lifted the gigantic plastic cup in front of him and took a polite sip of water. "He thinks it'll be too much of a distraction."

"And what do you think?" Ariana asked. She stole a glance at the ugly, neon-lit clock on the far side of the diner. If they hurried, she could be back on campus and with Thomas in half an hour.

He shrugged. "Don't know. It's gonna be a rough semester. Taking orgo and biology at the same time is really gonna blow. So maybe my dad is right." He laced his fingers together on the table and flashed her a mischievous smile. "He was right about you, anyway."

"Hmmm?" Ariana tipped her head slightly to the side. A loose lock of hair fell across her face, and Daniel reached over to brush it away. "What did he say about me?"

"He loved you." Daniel beamed. "Both my parents did. They wouldn't get off my case. Kept asking why I hadn't brought you home sooner." He reached for her hand. "And they really loved your accent." He grinned.

"Works like a charm," she said in an exaggerated southern drawl, warmth crawling from her neck into her cheeks. "I really liked them, too," she lied.

"They want to get your parents to Southampton some time in August." Daniel's eyes widened as he realized his mistake. "I mean, your mom. Or your dad. Whatever." He cleared his throat and pressed his palms into his wool pants. "Do they, like, ever do stuff together?" he hedged.

Ariana's face burned with embarrassment. "Occasionally."

Very occasionally, she added silently.

She felt the familiar protective walls rising around her, and it did not feel good. She'd been so open about her parents with Thomas that she had to remind herself to be guarded with Daniel. He would never understand—not that she even wanted him to.

"Well, I'm sure they'd do *this*," Daniel said. "I mean, if they knew how important it was to you."

Not important at all, you mean? Ariana thought wryly.

"I'm sure," she said.

"Good. Anyway, my parents asked how serious we were. They wanted to know what our plans were for next year." He looked relieved to be changing the subject, but as far as Ariana was concerned, this one wasn't any better.

Ariana bristled. "What did you tell them?"

She had to concentrate to keep from tugging at the neck of her sweater. It felt like the diner was getting warmer with every passing second. Like it was a giant oven, and someone was slowly turning up the heat. Torturing her.

"I told them we'd make it work long-distance, and that you'd probably spend most weekends up in Cambridge." He paused, searching her face. "I told them I loved you."

Weekends in Cambridge? They'd never discussed how they would handle next year. She *already* had a plan for next year, and it didn't involve Daniel.

"I love you, too." The words sounded cold, mechanical, coming from her mouth. But Daniel didn't seem to notice.

"Then it's settled," he said smugly.

Vomit. Barf. Heave.

Ariana imagined Thomas laughing at her inner dialogue and tried not to smile.

"Oh. And I also told my parents that you were unbelievable in bed," he said, deadpan. "In fact, maybe we should head back to my bed right now. It so needs to be christened."

Already taken care of, Ariana thought wryly. Thomas would have *loved* it if she said that out loud.

"What do you think?" Daniel asked.

"Daniel!" she hissed, feigning offense.

"Sorry. Couldn't resist," he said with a wolfish smile.

Ariana clucked her tongue and shook her head, which was exactly what the old her would have done. What she really wanted to do was tell him she knew all about his conquest list and smack him across the face. But she couldn't. Not yet. Instead, she watched him over the top of her menu as he looked around for a waitress.

Daniel was such an idiot. He believed that she loved him, and that she'd still been a virgin when she'd slept with him over break. Having sex with him had put her in control, and he didn't even know it. He was the naïve one. Not her.

"Does anybody work here?" he said to Ariana. He sighed in frustration. "Doesn't matter. I'll be right back and then we can order."

He slid out of the booth and ambled over to the restroom. Ariana watched him go with a smirk. She loved being in control.

She felt someone lingering next to the booth, and she glanced up to see a tall, pretty brunette staring down at her.

"Hi. I'll have a small salad and a tea, but I'm not sure what he wants," Ariana said, glancing toward the bathroom.

The girl smiled condescendingly. "I'm not your waitress, Ariana," she said. "But if I had to guess what your boyfriend wants, I'd say it'd probably be a girlfriend who doesn't cheat on him the second he turns his back."

"What?" Ariana's blood ran cold. Okay, there was no way she'd just heard the girl correctly. The diner was loud and crowded, and the girl must have somehow mistaken her for someone else. That was the only explanation. But how had she known Ariana's name?

"What? You don't agree?" the girl said blithely. Her voice was gravelly. Distinctive.

Ariana opened her mouth to speak, but the only sound that escaped was a sort of dry, strangled cough. She pressed her palms against her seat to steady herself. But her hands were slick with sweat, and they slid from the vinyl surface.

The girl lowered herself into Daniel's seat. "He's going to hurt you," she said simply.

Her words sliced through Ariana like a sharpened blade. She studied the girl's face: the gray eyes, the smooth, pale skin, the glossy brown hair that tumbled around her shoulders. Despite her pretty face, the girl had a harder edge than most Easton students. She wore a leather bomber jacket and an old wool cap. A threadbare navy scarf peeked out from under her collar.

Ariana steeled herself, faking nonchalance. Pretending that the very sight of this girl, the sound of her voice, didn't send chills down her spine. They both knew better.

"I can handle myself with Daniel," Ariana said.

"I'm not talking about Daniel. I'm talking about Thomas." The girl laced her fingers together on the table and leaned forward. A red, angry cut ran the length of her right hand. "I'm starting to think you're not as smart as everyone says."

"Thomas?" The room started to spin around her. She'd heard that voice before, but where? She tried desperately to place it. But her mind had gone blank with fear.

"He's not who you think he is," the girl said quietly. "Even if he did make you pancakes or light candles to keep you warm at night." She was staring right through Ariana with those glassy gray eyes. "Even if he promises to keep your secrets."

Ariana's mouth was completely dry, as if someone had filled it with sawdust. She tried to swallow but couldn't. What did this girl know? And how did she know it? Ariana raised her hand to the subway token again

"Of course, *I* never made that promise." The girl chuckled to herself, flicking her hair over one shoulder.

Ariana flinched. Was that a threat? Was this girl going to hurt her? Or worse, hurt Thomas? She cast a frantic glance toward the restrooms. Her first instinct was to search for Daniel. To find someone, anyone, who could protect her. But she stopped herself. Daniel could never, ever find out about this girl. She knew too much. More than too much. She knew *everything*.

But how?

"Don't bother," the girl said smoothly, without turning around. "I'll be gone before he gets back."

Ariana felt as if someone had bound and gagged her. She was mute, powerless. At the mercy of this stranger. She swallowed the thick lump in her throat.

"Who are you?" she finally managed, her voice strained and unfamiliar. She was definitely no longer in control. She tried to fight the nausea that rose up in her stomach. This wasn't happening. It wasn't possible. The nightmare was supposed to be over, dealt with. "What do you want?"

"It doesn't matter who I am. But what I want is Thomas," the girl snapped. Suddenly, her eyes were ablaze with light. It was as if the very mention of Thomas's name had brought her to life. Ariana clutched her own arm under the table, held on for dear life. "And he used to want me. Everything was perfect. We loved each other. And then one day, he told me that he still loved me, but that things were too complicated between us." She blinked, her eyes boring through Ariana. "And then he found you."

Ariana shook her head slowly. This girl wasn't making any sense. Sure, Thomas had a reputation on campus, a reputation for getting around. But this girl definitely wasn't an Easton student. Ariana didn't recognize her face. But that voice . . .

"I always knew I was going to get him back." A faint, faraway smile surfaced on the girl's lips. "You're just a blip. We were meant for each other."

The girl was insane. "Thomas is with me now," Ariana said, trying to keep her voice level. She slipped her hand into her bag, and her fingers closed around a pen. "Not you."

"That's what you think," the girl said, laughing strangely. "But you're going to stay away from him. Unless you want your other boyfriend to find out about what you've been up to."

Ariana said nothing, gripping the pen so tightly that her hand began to tingle, numbness slipping over it.

"You remember, don't you? All those things you did. Things that I'm sure Daniel would be very interested in. The sex . . ." The girl shook her head slowly. "The murder. That poor boy," she murmured. "The police would probably appreciate an anonymous tip as to exactly who he was with out on that lake and exactly how he 'drowned.'"

"How do you know all this?" Ariana's voice was barely audible.

"I keep my eyes open," the girl replied. "Of course, it's completely up to you whether I go to the cops or not." The girl leaned across the table, her cold eyes just inches away. "Just remember—you're on thin ice. And, if memory serves, that's a dangerous place to be."

She leaned back, laughing at her sick, twisted joke. As she stood up, she tugged a scarf out of her jacket collar with her cut-up hand and wound it around her neck. A dark navy argyle scarf.

Ariana gasped, recognizing the fabric.

"Stay away from him," she said under her breath, resting her hand on Ariana's shoulder. She squeezed tight, digging her nails into Ariana's skin. "I won't ask you again."

And then she was gone.

Ariana sank, lifeless, into the booth. Within seconds, the realization of what had just happened sank in. Her hands started to tremble, then her arms, her legs, her feet. Soon, her entire body was shaking, racked with fear and guilt and shame.

That girl had a dark navy argyle scarf. Just like in the picture of her and Thomas kissing in Daniel's room. The argyle material swam before her eyes as heat surged through her body. Sergei hadn't taken the picture of Ariana and Thomas. Now that she thought about it, the picture of her and Thomas kissing in Daniel's room hadn't even been on his camera. How could have she been so stupid? He hadn't been the one screwing with their minds, making Easton's campus a living hell.

Suddenly, Ariana couldn't breathe. All she could hear were Sergei's pleas. Him asking her to help him. Begging her. Saw his eyes go blank as he sank beneath the surface of the lake.

It hadn't been him. But he had died anyway. Murdered. Ariana had murdered him for no good reason.

No. No, no, no.

It had all been for nothing.

She clawed at the neck of her sweater and fumbled for the water glass in front of her, knocking it clear off the table. The family at the counter turned to stare.

In . . . two . . . three . . .

Out . . . two . . . three . . .

In . . . two . . . three . . .

Out . . . two . . . three . . .

Just then, the waitress rushed over with napkins. "Are you okay, hon?"

"Fine. Thanks," Ariana lied. "I just remembered I have someplace to be." She had to get out of the diner. Now. Any second Daniel was going to return from the bathroom and catch her in the middle of this panic attack. She couldn't have that. She had to go. Ariana grabbed her coat and stumbled into the street. She gulped the winter air as if she were fighting to keep her head above water. As if she were about to get pulled beneath the surface again.

Her world was starting to crumble. She could feel it. Everything she'd worked so hard to keep, everything she deserved, was slipping from her grasp. And she didn't know how to hold on any tighter.

THE TRUTH

Ariana waited patiently in the dark of Thomas's room until he returned. After thinking for hours about what had happened at the diner, mulling it over and twisting it around, her brain had finally started to clear. Sergei was not her fault. That girl was responsible. She was there. She could have stopped Ariana. Could have told her Sergei was innocent. She was the one with Sergei's blood on her hands. Plus, Sergei *had* known about her and Thomas. Would always have been a threat. But those realizations didn't solve all of Ariana's problems.

"Who is she?" she asked quietly when he opened the door. Pale light from the hallway leaked across the floor, illuminating tiny shards of jagged glass embedded in the floor planks. The broken Captain Morgan's bottle still sat on Thomas's desk. Reminding her.

"What the—" Thomas flipped the light switch on the wall and whirled around. He collapsed against the door when he saw Ariana sitting cross-legged on his bed, still wearing her coat and scarf. "Jesus,

Ariana. You scared the crap out of me." He dropped his athletic bag and basketball next to the door, looking relieved. "What are you doing here?"

"I asked you first. Who is she?" she repeated evenly, staring him down. Despite the fact that Ketlar was heated again, a slick cold crept over her skin.

"Who's who? I don't know what you're talking about," he said, hovering nervously near the door.

"So I'll refresh your memory," she said coolly. She had trusted Thomas like she'd never trusted anyone before. She had given him her virginity, and in return, he had hidden something from her. That was going to stop. Now. If they were going to get through this together, she had to know everything. "Tall brunette. Pretty. Says she loved you, and you dumped her without any warning." Emotion started to creep into her voice, and she swallowed it. This wasn't the time to let her feelings get in the way. Feelings only complicated things.

Slowly, the color drained from Thomas's face. "I—I don't know who you're talking about."

Liar.

"Wrong," Ariana said calmly, running her fingers over the worn plaid bedspread beneath her. "Try again." Her voice was flat. No hint of the rage that boiled inside her.

"Ariana, I swear—"

"Don't lie to me!" Ariana shouted, standing.

Thomas took a step back "All right!" he whispered. "All right. Just keep it down."

Ariana crossed her arms over her chest and waited. Waited while Thomas ran his hands through his hair. Composed what he was going to say.

"Her name is Melissa," he said weakly. He ambled across the room and slumped against his desk. "Mel Johnston. I dated her for a while this fall." He paused, glancing warily in Ariana's direction as he unbuttoned his coat and tossed it on his bed.

Ariana was silent.

"I met her through some of my friends at Easton High," he continued. "We went out for a few months and she got kinda clingy, so I broke it off. No big deal. Please don't—"

"When?" she asked icily. "When did you break it off?" The sound of Thomas begging only made her angrier. It made him seem weak.

"I don't know." He stuffed his hands in his pockets and looked down at the floor, studying it as if seeing it for the very first time. "Maybe a month ago? She didn't take it too well, and I haven't heard from her since." He looked up at Ariana, a pleading gaze burning in his sapphire eyes. "Listen. It's over. I swear. I didn't tell you because I didn't think it was a big deal. I don't know why it's so important—"

"Because she *knows*, Thomas!" Ariana exploded, lunging in his direction. "She knows everything!"

He recoiled into his desk, knocking the broken bottle to the floor. The rest of it shattered, sending splintered pieces of glass to the far corners of the small room.

"What?" Thomas's voice was thick with fear. "What the hell are you talking about?"

"She saw us together," Ariana spat, trying desperately to keep her voice down. If anyone heard her screaming and caught her in Thomas's room, they were screwed. "She knows we had sex. She knows about Sergei." Tears welled up in her eyes at the very sound of that name. "And she told me that if I didn't stay away from you, she was going to tell Daniel everything. She said she'd go to the police." The weight of the threat was palpable, heavy in the air. "The *police*, Thomas."

"Oh my God." Thomas rubbed his face with both hands, exhaling slowly. "Okay. Give me a second to think." He jumped down from his desk, pacing back and forth in front of the bed. Head down. Glass crunched under his every step. "How did you . . ." he started. "Where did she find you?"

"In town."

Ariana suddenly felt drained. Every last bit of strength had been sapped from her body. It took everything she had just to breathe. In and out. One breath at a time. She collapsed onto Thomas's bed, inhaling the scent of his pillow. But even his familiar smell couldn't comfort her now.

Eyes closed, she took a deep breath and told him everything this Mel girl had said—except, of course, exactly how Sergei had died.

"She's serious, Thomas," Ariana said quietly, wishing she could sink into the mattress and disappear. "I can tell."

"Crazy bitch." Thomas stared at the floor for a while. "How the hell did she even know about us?"

"I don't know, but she was following us all weekend," Ariana said. "I'm surprised she and Sergei didn't bump into each other in the—"

Suddenly the truth rushed in on Ariana. It hit her so hard her brain went foggy for a moment. But when it cleared again, she was sure. She knew exactly how Mel had found out about them.

"The North Face store," she said quietly.

"What?" Thomas said.

"She was in the store that night. When I was shopping for Daniel and you . . . surprised me," Ariana said, her heart pounding. "I remember her voice. You were about to kiss me and then—"

Thomas's face lit with understanding.

"Holy crap. She's the one who knocked into the rack and stopped us."

"I knew I recognized her voice. She said she was sorry," Ariana said. "That must have been the first time she saw us."

"How did you recognize her voice tonight, but I didn't even notice in the store?" Thomas asked.

"I have a thing for details," Ariana said quickly. "Who cares? The question is, what are we going to do?"

"I don't know. I don't know," Thomas said. Anger and panic were beginning to creep into his voice, and the glass crunched more loudly, more insistently under his feet as he crisscrossed the room. "If she tells, I'll lose everything. Easton, my inheritance." He stopped abruptly in front of his door and slammed his fist into it.

"Thomas!" Ariana jumped off the bed and grabbed his arm before he could swing again. She ignored the small voice in the back of her mind telling her Thomas hadn't said he couldn't lose her. "Stop it!" She gripped his sweater, trying to pull him away. He shrugged her off, but she ducked between his body and the door, blocking him. Taking his hand, she saw that tiny drops of blood had surfaced on his knuckles.

She held his gaze, held onto the connection between them like a rapidly fraying thread. She could feel him pulling away, pulling back from her. And it was all because of Mel. She was to blame.

"It's my fault," he said, his voice cracking. "This whole thing is my fault."

"No." Ariana cupped her hands around the back of his neck. It was drenched with sweat. "Don't. Don't say that."

"Why shouldn't I?" Thomas snapped, pulling away. His upper lip twitched slightly. "It's true, isn't it? None of this would be happening if I hadn't screwed her over. I can't lose Easton. I can't."

Thomas took a deep breath and looked at Ariana. She could see his breathing start to normalize and she felt a flutter of pride. He trusted her, loved her. She was capable of calming him. He was just upset because he knew Mel could ruin everything for both of them.

"We have to do something," Ariana said firmly. "We have to stop her."

"What can we do?" Thomas said. "The girl's nuts. You said she wants you to stay away from me, right?"

"Right."

"So we just make sure she doesn't see us together." He tilted his head toward her. Reached out to touch her hand. "We were going to be apart this year, anyway. Now we have to be even more careful when we meet up."

He was trying to reassure her, but it wasn't enough. They had planned to lie low for the rest of the year, but they had also planned to be together next year, after Daniel was gone. Why wasn't Thomas worried about next year? Why didn't he want to make sure that Mel never had the chance to turn them in? Ariana turned toward him, looked into his eyes. They were blank; she couldn't read him.

"So that takes care of this year," she began. "But what about—"

She felt him flinch slightly, and she froze. It would have been imperceptible to anyone else. But not to her. She already knew him well enough to know his every move. She knew him well enough to know that he would never be with her as long as Mel was in the picture. He knew that Mel could hurt them, and he wanted to protect Ariana. Protect her because he loved her. But protecting her meant pulling away. And she couldn't let that happen.

Deep calm settled over her, soothing her burning nerves. She started toward the door.

"Where are you going?" Thomas jumped up after her.

"I have to get back to Billings," she said simply. "Noelle's going to start wondering where I am. Or worse, Paige."

"Okay," he said. "See you later?"

"Sure."

"Wait." Thomas gripped her arm, pulling her back. "You okay?"

She opened the door and peered into the hallway. It was empty.

"I'm fine," she said reassuringly. And she was. But he wasn't. He looked so worried, so scared. So fragile. And in that instant she knew she was the only one who could ever take care of him the way he needed. The only one who could make sure he didn't break.

And after all, wasn't that what it was to be in love?

PEACE

Ariana gripped the chain-link fence and marveled at how well the gloves Noelle had given her kept out the cold. Squinting into the heavy fog, she stared at the large double doors that loomed at the top of several sets of rambling steps. A large stone archway carved with the words EASTON HIGH SCHOOL, EST. 1935 crumbled over the doors. Moss had crept into the crevices of the letters, giving them a greenish tinge. With the exception of a ragged American flag whipping in the wind, the school grounds were bare. Silent.

A loud car drove by—silver, four-door, broken muffler— and Ariana checked her watch. Just then the harsh clanging of the afternoon bell echoed in the halls and around the deserted grounds. Seconds later, the doors flew open and waves of students poured down the steps. She blocked out the noise that flooded the yard as they spilled into the street. Settled into the quiet calm of her mind, searching the crowds for a familiar face. This time would be different. This time, she would be the one catching Mel off guard.

Ariana almost didn't see her, hunched over in jeans and the same leather jacket she'd worn the day before. The same dark scarf secured around her long neck. Mel crossed her arms over her chest and took the stairs two at a time, keeping her head down. Instinctively, Ariana turned away as Mel slipped through the high gates. The other students huddled together in groups, laughing and talking. Mel stayed by herself, ducking through the patches of students without acknowledging them. Ariana watched as Mel moved quickly down the sidewalk, sidestepping the weeds in the cracked cement.

"Hey!"

Ariana looked up, startled. A tall kid in camouflage pants was blocking her path. An unlit cigarette hung limp between his lips. A group of a few guys stood behind him, smirking in her direction.

"What?" she snapped, keeping her eye on Mel. The distance between them was widening fast. She felt her heart throbbing in her chest. She couldn't lose her. This was her chance.

"Got a light?" the kid sneered, stepping closer.

"No." Ariana shook her head, staring past him. "I don't smoke."

"No big deal." He pulled the cigarette from between his lips and stuffed it in his pocket. "You new around here?"

"Kind of." Mel was crossing the street, cutting through the gas station parking lot on the corner. If Ariana didn't move fast, she was going to lose sight of her. She shoved past the group of guys. The sharp sound of her heels pounding against the cement overpowered the laughter and shouts behind her. She sprinted across the street and slowed as she reached the parking lot. Mel wasn't far ahead.

Ariana hung back, her heartbeat thundering in her ears.

A few blocks from the gas station, Mel crossed the street again, heading down a tiny side street peppered with small, run-down houses. She unlatched the gate in front of the last house on the street and made her way up the steps to the front door. Ariana hid behind a tree at the edge of the yard, watching her.

Mel shrugged off her backpack and fished around inside it, pulling out a single key. She wedged her body between a ripped screen door and the front door, and inserted the key into the lock. Relief enveloped Ariana, and she sank back against the rough bark of the tree with a small smile.

The girl was alone.

As soon as the screen door slammed shut, Ariana slipped across the yard. Closed her gloved hand around the rusted doorknob and took a slow, deep breath. There was only one thing that stood between her and Thomas Pearson. One thing that threatened the happiness she'd found.

She shook her head as she twisted the doorknob slowly. Thomas had left Mel, but she actually believed they could still be together. Believed that they were meant for each other. She refused to accept the fact that it was over. That Thomas loved Ariana, wanted her. He had made that clear, but Mel was too blinded by her own obsession to see it.

Ariana almost felt sorry for the girl.

The old wooden door creaked slowly as she pushed it open. She blinked the moment she stepped into the entryway, her eyes adjusting to the blackness that wavered in front of her. It closed in on her. She raised her hand just inches in front of her face, but she couldn't see a thing. Sliding her hands against the wall next to her, she moved slowly though the foyer.

Suddenly, the door slammed behind her. Ariana's heart surged. She closed her eyes and strained to hear the sound of Mel's voice. Her footsteps. But she heard nothing except for the low hum of heat filtering through the radiators. And the sound of her own voice in her head. Willing her body to do what had to be done.

Silently, Ariana pressed her body against the wall, sweat dripping from her face to her neck, down the length of her body. Blood thundered in her ears, flooding through her veins at high speed. The wall suddenly gave from behind her, and she whirled around. She was standing in a long hallway. The carpet was taupe, worn—cheap looking. A smile twitched at the corners of her mouth as she saw a closed bedroom door at the end of it. Light spilled from underneath the door, as if to guide her down the hall.

She held her breath as she headed toward the room. In the gray light that drenched the hall, she hurried past family photographs that hung on either side of her. Baby pictures, wedding pictures. A stiff, posed photograph of Mel—probably a school portrait. Ariana kept her head down. When she reached the doorway, she gripped the knob so tightly it made her gloved hand hurt.

Pulling the door open slowly, she stepped into a room that looked strangely similar to her side of the room in Billings. It was perfectly neat. Next to the door, a worn dresser was covered with a few framed photographs and a black plastic top hat with the glittering words HAPPY NEW YEAR printed on it. A desk with only a desktop computer on it was wedged next to the closet.

Across the room, Mel lay on a double bed covered with a violet blanket and a few throw pillows. Her eyes were closed, and a long leg tumbled over the side of the bed, her foot tapping the carpeted floor to the beat of the guitar music that leaked from her earbuds. A single lamp glowed on the bedside table next to the bed.

Ariana closed the door behind her. The lock echoed with a satisfactory *click*, and she crossed the room and stood at the edge of Mel's bed. She noticed a picture on the bedside table, a picture she hadn't been able to see from the doorway. Rage churned inside her as she looked closer. It was a picture of Thomas. His soccer picture. He was kneeling on the field in his uniform, his soccer ball wedged under one arm. Ariana chewed the flesh on the inside of her cheek to keep from screaming. She leaned over the bed, her body casting a shadow over Mel's form.

Mel's eyelids flickered and opened, widening in horror as Ariana clamped her hand over Mel's mouth. Dulling the scream that shook Mel's body. She ripped the tiny white earbuds out of Mel's ears and tossed the iPod on the floor. The music continued to blare from across the room. Mel thrashed under Ariana's grip.

"Shut up," Ariana snapped. "Shut up and I'll let go. I just want to talk to you."

Mel nodded silently, her body deflating into the blanket beneath her.

Ariana removed her hand slowly, taking a step back from the bed. "Don't move," she warned.

"What do you want?" Mel snapped. She scrambled to the corner of her bed closest to the wall, squinting at Ariana with her dark gray eyes. Ariana could tell she was trying to look angry. But instead of anger, Ariana saw something else. Raw fear. Her lips curved into a half smile. Her body felt completely relaxed, drained of any tension or anger she'd felt toward the girl before. She was calm, collected.

Because Mel was afraid. And that fear put Ariana in control.

"I think you know what I want," she said lightly. "I want Thomas. But you were going to take him away from me." She reached over to the lamp on Mel's bedside table. It was cracked in several places, and she traced the cracks slowly, deliberately, with the tip of her index finger, the cashmere gloves occasionally catching on the tiny nicks. "I think we both know I can't let that happen, Melissa."

Mel's body was heaving now, her face reddening. "You stole him," she said, her deep voice getting progressively louder over the sound of the shriek of a guitar solo radiating from the earbuds on the floor. "He's mine, and—"

"Not anymore," Ariana said sharply, cutting her off. "He's not yours anymore. He'd never want you back after everything you did to him. Everything you did to us." Her pulse was starting to race again, and she paused, willing herself to calm down. Evened her breathing. "Stalking us, blackmailing us, stealing that picture of me—"

"That wasn't me," Mel said frantically, gripping her blanket in her fists. Pressing her back against the wall. "That boy. He broke into your room and stole the picture. I watched him do it."

"Liar." Ariana hissed. "Sergei was innocent. He never did anything to hurt you. And you killed him."

"*I* killed him?" Mel laughed, looking Ariana boldly in the eye. "Sounds like you've forgotten the most important part of the story, Ariana. The part where he begged *you* for his life. Begged *you* to help him. The part where you shoved him under. And the part where you lied to Thomas about it. So I'd be careful who I called a liar, if I were you."

Mel's suddenly composed demeanor sent jolts of fury through Ariana. She'd only lied to Thomas to because she had to. Only shielded him from the knowledge of how Sergei had died. Protected him. Her hands began to tremble.

"You think Thomas will want you when he finds out about what you did to that boy?" Mel barked, leaning forward on the bed. "You think he wants to be with a murderer?" She dove toward Ariana, a wild look in her eye. "He'll leave you! Just like he left me!"

"No!" Ariana reached for the lamp on the bedside table, wrapping her fist around its base. The cord ripped from the wall as Ariana lunged toward the bed and the room was plunged was into darkness.

In an instant it was all over, and once again Ariana was at peace.

I-L-L-E-G-A-L

"I heard about what happened," Isobel whispered to Ariana in the middle of Mr. Holmes's class the next day. Her sleek dark locks tumbled over her face. "About what you did over break?" Her green eyes were wide, disbelieving.

A sudden chill ran through Ariana's body. Isobel couldn't know. It was impossible. There wasn't a single living soul who knew what had happened; Ariana had made sure of that. But Ariana knew Isobel's dirty little secret; was it possible that Isobel knew hers? She kept her gazed fixed straight ahead. Mr. Holmes was gesturing toward the chalkboard, but she didn't hear a word he was saying.

"I don't know what you're talking about," she whispered back, sneaking a glance down the semicircle of chairs to see if Paige could hear anything from her perch a few seats away. Paige was too busy texting on her BlackBerry to notice.

Connie Tolson leaned forward in her seat and flashed Ariana a death stare.

"Please," Isobel said, narrowing her eyes knowingly in Ariana's direction. "Don't play innocent with me, Ariana. Noelle told me everything."

Noelle? Ariana was starting to feel faint. True, Noelle was always the first to know everything that happened on campus. True, she always seemed to know exactly what Ariana was thinking, feeling. But she had been so careful. Tied up every last loose end. She wrapped her arms around her body, curling into herself.

"Noelle knows?"

Isobel nodded. "I met her for drinks at Platinum at the end of break. Only took one-point-five dirty martinis to get her to spill." She leaned closer. "Those things are brutal," she giggled. Her thick Anna Sui perfume invaded the space around them, and Ariana was overcome with a wave of nausea. "So," Isobel continued, flashing a devilish grin. "How'd you do it?"

Ariana's head snapped toward her in disbelief. How could she be so blasé? She noticed Mr. Holmes looking in her direction, and she opened her alligator clutch, pretending to search for a pen.

"I think my first time was missionary," Isobel said with a thoughtful hair toss. "With Jordan Krauss? He graduated last year. A little boring. But I pretty much just had to lie there and let him do all the work."

Relief rushed over Ariana like a warm Caribbean breeze in the dead of winter. "You're talking about Daniel and me?" she whispered.

"Fine." Isobel smiled. "Play dumb for now. But I want the whole story later."

Ariana smiled in return, her heart beating normally again.

"Miss Osgood?" Mr. Holmes was looking directly at her, an amused look in his eye. "I hope I'm not interrupting anything?"

"No," she said weakly.

She looked down at her lap, her cheeks burning. Of course he had called her out in front of the whole class without so much as acknowledging that Isobel had been talking too. Apparently whatever Isobel had learned from Jordan Krauss was good enough to get her immunity for the rest of the semester.

"Good." He nodded, loosening his tie. "I was just saying that we'll start on Hugo's *Les Misérables* next week. Be ready to discuss the foreword and the first five chapters." He walked around the edge of his desk and pulled a thick manila envelope from his bag. "That should do it for today, folks," he announced, unwinding the thin string that held the envelope closed. "Once you've gotten your *Madame Bovary* papers back, you're free to go." He dumped the stack on his desk and pulled the first paper from the pile. "Aldridge?"

"So what did you do over break?" Ariana turned to Isobel as chatter in the classroom swelled around them. "Anything good?"

"My break wasn't as exciting as yours, that's for sure." Isobel snickered. "I got bangs cut." She fingered the heavy fringe that fell across her forehead. "Other than that, I was stuck going to a lot of dinner parties with my parents once they got back from vacation. The only thing that got me through it was the fact that Jack was visiting." She lowered her voice, a half smile playing across her lips. "Funny how a quickie in the coat closet during the salad course will get you through dessert and coffee." She laughed, pulling a tin of lip balm from her clutch.

"Funny," Ariana echoed, watching Isobel dip her ring finger into the sticky gloss and apply it expertly to her smooth pout. "Anything else?"

Isobel looked up at her. Innocence radiated from her pores, thicker than her perfume. "Not really."

Ariana tried to mask the disgust that crept through her as she watched Isobel check her reflection in her compact mirror. Isobel Bautista was the perfect example of everything that was wrong with Easton Academy. Flawless on the outside. But what was hidden beneath her shiny veneer was imperfect. Ugly.

"Osgood." Mr. Holmes tossed Ariana's paper on her desk, and she caught it just before it fell to the floor. She flipped it over and stared at the large red marks on the cover sheet. C-plus. She clenched her jaw as the letter swam in front of her.

"Ready to go?" Isobel snapped her compact shut and stood up.

"What about yours?" Ariana stared numbly at her desk.

"Got an A," she replied, tucking a few sheets of paper into her bag. She laughed to herself and tugged her plum-colored Miu Miu coat on over her scarf. "Want to get out of here and get some coffee?"

"I could use a latte." Paige appeared behind Isobel, wearing tan ankle boots and the new low-cut sweater dress she'd bought over break.

"Great," Isobel chirped. "Ariana was going to tell us all about her naughty little vacation." A few seconds too late, her manicured hand flew to her mouth. "Oops."

Ariana's cheeks flushed.

"Spare me the details, will you, Isobel?" Paige sneered, without looking at Ariana. "That's my brother you're talking about."

"I— I wasn't thinking," Isobel stuttered.

"Shocker." Paige yawned. "Let's get out of here."

Ariana lowered her gaze to the paper in her hands. *C+.* This couldn't be right. She'd never made anything less than an A-minus in her entire life. And Mr. Holmes was supposed to be an easy grader. Anger rose in her chest. She couldn't let him get away with this. It wasn't fair.

"Ariana?" Isobel rested her hand on Ariana's sleeve.

"You guys go on," she mumbled. "I have to ask Mr. Holmes something."

Isobel raised a perfectly arched eyebrow. "You want us to wait?"

Ariana shook her head. "I'll meet you back at Billings."

"Fine." Paige's phone buzzed, and she pressed it to her ear, hurrying out of the classroom.

"Don't be long," Isobel teased. "As soon as you're done, I want the filthy play-by-play."

Ariana forced a laugh. It sounded strange, guttural, in her own ears. "You'll get it, I swear."

"That's my girl."

She wedged her clutch underneath her arm and sashayed up the aisle. Pausing briefly in front of Mr. Holmes's desk, she ran her fingertip seductively along the sleek wood before flouncing out the door. She thought she was so clever. They both did. Thought they were getting away with something. They couldn't have been more wrong.

Ariana waited for the last of the students to take their papers and dribble out the door and into the hallway. Quietly, she slipped into her trench, gathered her books, and headed for the front of the room. Mr. Holmes was hunched over the crossword puzzle, muttering something to himself. She stood in front of his desk, looking down at him. Waiting. After a few minutes, he looked up.

"Miss Osgood." He looked genuinely surprised to see her. "You didn't happen to stay behind to give me a six-letter word for 'precious jewels,' did you?" He smiled, tucking his pen into his shirt pocket.

"Bijoux." Ariana let her paper slip from her grip. It fluttered to his desk, landing on top of the newspaper. "You gave me a C-plus."

Mr. Holmes exhaled slowly, leaning back in his chair. "You deserved a C-plus," he said, flipping through the pages. "This wasn't your best work, Ariana," he said gently. "You're better than this. We both know that. But I had to be fair."

"Fair?" She laughed bitterly. Reached into her purse, her hand closing around a cell phone. She ran her fingers slowly over the keys, happy in the knowledge that she had the power to get exactly what she deserved.

He nodded. "I know you'll show me something better on *Les Misérables*, and don't worry about it. You still got an A for the first semester." He smiled warmly, interlacing his hands together in his lap. "Any other questions?"

She nodded, pulling his phone from her bag. "I was just wondering . . ." she began as shock and surprise passed briefly over his features. Her fingers flew across the keys, and she tilted the screen toward him, holding it just out of his reach. "What's a seven-letter word for sex with a seventeen-year-old student?" She pressed the button on the side of the phone and smiled at the sound of Mr. Holmes moaning Isobel's name.

"Stop." His voice was strained. Desperate. "Turn that off. Now."

"But we were just getting to the good part." She paused the video, batting her eyelashes at him. "Oh. I've got it," she announced sweetly, tilting her head to the side. "I-L-L-E-G-A-L."

The color had drained completely from Mr. Holmes's face. "Where did you get that?" He was trying to sound stern, but his voice wavered with fear.

"Does it matter?"

He shook his head slowly. "No. Of course not."

He pulled a pen from his pocket and lowered his shaking hand to her paper. Deliberately, he crossed out the C+ and scrawled a large, red A across the center of the page. He didn't even look at her as he handed the paper back. But she never once took her eyes off him.

"Thank you. I assume you'll update your grade book as well?" she said with a smile.

"Of course."

"By the way, for what it's worth, I really enjoyed the book." She stuffed the paper into her bag. "It taught me a lot."

"Good." He nodded, still looking down. "I'm glad. Anything else I can help you with?"

"That's all for now." She hovered over his desk for a few moments more, daring him to look her in the eye. He didn't. "But I'll let you know."

She dropped the phone into her bag. Before she stepped into the hallway, she stole one last glance at Mr. Holmes. He was hunched over his desk, raking his hands through his hair. Destroyed. But she didn't feel the slightest bit guilty. He'd gotten exactly what he deserved.

STUPID

Ariana hurried toward Mitchell Hall later that night, just minutes before Mr. Barber's world history class was supposed to end. Her chest rose and fell in anticipation as she ran up the stairs and threw open the doors. The hallway was empty, and she could hear the muffled sounds of scraping chairs and laughter coming from the end of the hall. Her timing was perfect. She slowed to a stroll—a Billings Girl couldn't be caught running in the halls—and stopped outside the last doorway on the left.

The door was open a crack, and she felt a flood of warmth as she heard Thomas's voice leaking from the classroom. He'd be so happy when she told him. Told him that she'd taken care of everything, that their plan was no longer in jeopardy.

They could still be together in the fall. No one would stand in their way.

She wound a lock of hair around her index finger and smiled. She had it all figured out. Finally, her life was unfolding the way it was meant to unfold. Thomas was her happily-ever-after.

The classroom door opened, and Ariana ducked out of the way. Students shoved past one another into the hallway. She flattened herself against the wall, hoping to catch a glimpse of Thomas in the crowd. Finally, she saw him, a soccer ball wedged under his arm. He tossed the ball up above his head and the kid behind him swiped it out of the air.

"Give it back, asshole." Thomas laughed, shoving the kid against the wall. He grabbed the ball and hung back while the rest of the class continued down the hallway. In one smooth movement, he dropped the ball to the floor, dribbling it slowly toward the double doors.

Ariana loved watching Thomas. There was a vulnerability in him that no one at Easton had ever really seen. To them, he was the player, the elusive bad boy. Just another entitled kid with a screwed-up family. But Ariana saw the real Thomas Pearson. She saw it in the way his face relaxed completely when he slept, and in the way he stuffed his hands in his pockets when he got nervous. In the way he smiled to himself when he thought no one was watching.

She crept up behind him and covered his eyes with her hands.

"Guess who," she whispered, her lips close to his ear.

Thomas whirled around, surprised. "What are you doing?" He swooped down and lifted the soccer ball from the floor.

"If I didn't know better, I'd say you weren't happy to see me," Ariana said, her shoulders tensing.

"It's not that." He took her wrist and tugged her into an empty classroom, closing the door behind them. When he turned to look at her, his expression was serious. His eyes darted to the slim window in the door as if he was afraid someone would peek in. "You need to be more careful. You know how fast gossip travels around this place. And now with Melissa . . . "

Ariana grinned. "I'm not worried about Melissa anymore."

Thomas blinked. "I'm confused. Yesterday you were all freaked about her."

"That was yesterday," Ariana said coolly, tracing her fingertip on the smooth surface of one of the oak desks, making a little heart. "As of today, your little girlfriend won't be bothering us anymore."

Thomas eyed her quizzically. He wasn't getting it.

"I took care of her," Ariana clarified.

She watched him carefully, waiting for the relief to surface in his expression. Instead, the muscles in his face tensed. His jaw clenched and Ariana felt the briefest flutter of uncertainty.

"What do you mean, you took care of her?" he asked, taking a small step backward. "What did you do, Ariana?"

Ariana stared at his muddy sneakers. Why had he stepped away? That one movement had thrown her completely. Taken her confidence.

"It doesn't matter," she said quickly, waving a hand. She stepped toward him, closing the space between them once more. "All that matters is that we can be together now. She can't hurt us anymore."

Ariana reached for him, but he flinched away. Her heart fell into her stomach like a stone, and tears instantly welled in her eyes. He was supposed to be relieved, not angry. He was supposed to be thankful. Ecstatic. Didn't he realize what she had done for him? For them?

"What the fuck did you do to her?" Thomas shouted, his voice cracking.

Ariana's heart stopped. For the first time, she felt scared of Thomas.

"I . . . I did what I had to do. She was going to ruin everything for us, Thomas. But now—"

"Did what you had to do? How *stupid* are you, Ariana?" Thomas blurted, shoving his hands into his hair. His face was contorted with fear and rage. "Who do you think they're going to come after? They're going to come after *me!*"

Ariana struggled for breath. She had never seen him so angry. So out of control. "No, they won't. I thought of that. I made sure you had an alibi. You were in class. Fifteen other people will be able to back you up."

Thomas glanced at her, his nostrils flared. "You're sure."

"I'm sure," she said, her pulse calming as he started to relax.

Thomas took a deep breath and blew it out, looking at the floor. "What about you? What's your alibi?"

"They won't ask me," Ariana said with a scoff. "I have no connection to the girl. She was just some townie."

"But what if they do, Ariana?" Thomas asked. "What if someone remembers seeing you two together that day she confronted you? What are you going to do?"

Ariana smiled. He was so concerned for her. He was just upset now because he was scared. Scared for her. For them. She knew he loved her.

"I was in the library with Noelle. I went to get a book and to check something online and came back an hour later, but she won't remember that. She'll just remember we studied together that day," Ariana said, lifting a palm. "Noelle will tell them I was with her."

Thomas nodded slowly, but he still kept his distance. How could he stand to be so far away?

"I did this for us, Thomas. You know that, right? Because if anyone ever figured out what we did over break, if Mel ever told . . . that would be the end. Of us. Of you at Easton. Of my mother."

It seemed to take forever for him to look at her. But when he did, his eyes were clear again. He understood. He understood her better than anyone. He knew she would stop at nothing to get what she wanted. She would stop at nothing to protect what they had.

He came to her, cupped her face with his hands, and looked into her eyes. "I'm sorry I overreacted. It's going to be okay."

Ariana went weightless with relief.

"So you're not mad?" Ariana asked. "We're going to stick to the plan?"

Thomas swallowed hard. There was something in his eyes that she couldn't quite place, so she chose to ignore it. "We're going to stick to the plan," he said firmly.

The certainty in his voice sent a pleasant, confident warmth through her veins.

"Good. Because I can't wait to be with you. In front of everyone," she said, closing her eyes and kissing him softly on the lips. "I love you, Thomas."

She waited for his response. And waited. Her heart started to shrink in on itself and she opened her eyes to look at him. He had been staring past her, but quickly focused on her face.

"I love you, too," he said.

Ariana breathed in. She knew it. She knew he loved her.

"And next year, when things are back to normal, we'll be together. For real." He twisted her gold chain around his finger and ran his thumb over the subway token he'd given her. "I swear."

Ariana nodded happily. Staring into his eyes, she unfastened the chain from around her neck, slipped the token off, and dropped it in Thomas's pocket. She didn't want Daniel asking questions about it, and Thomas could give it back to her in the fall, when she could wear it proudly. September seemed like it was eons away, but she didn't need to worry. Because she knew, deep down, that she and Thomas were meant for each other.

This wasn't the end. It was just the beginning.

Ariana stood motionless while the herd of students swept past her in the quad. They were all making their afternoon classes, laughing, texting, fiddling with BlackBerrys and iPods. And no one really saw her. It was as if she were part of the landscape. One of the silent, ancient campus buildings that held so many secrets.

"Ariana, are you coming?" Noelle asked.

"What?" Ariana blinked, startled out of her thoughts.

"If we're late, one of us runs the risk of having to kick off the whole 'what did you read over the summer' discussion. Hint?" Noelle batted her eyes sweetly. "It won't be me."

"I'll catch up with you," Ariana assured her.

Noelle narrowed her eyes and shrugged. "Your funeral." She turned on her heel and strolled through the quad, groups of lower-classmen parting in front of her like the Red Sea.

Ariana shook her head and sighed, scanning the crowd that was pouring through the cafeteria doors and into the sunshine. There were times when she felt that Noelle didn't really know her any better than anyone else at Easton. She'd felt the same way about Daniel when they'd been together last year. Had felt that no matter how many friends she had, no matter how many people surrounded her or how many girls wanted to be just like her, she was still alone. That no one saw her.

But then there was Thomas. He knew her. Really knew her. She could tell by the way he looked at her when they'd meet in Gwendolyn Hall. It was a mixture of intrigue and attraction. And love.

She'd had it all planned out in her mind—their big reunion, him sweeping her up in his arms, finally able to touch her in public. No more sneaking around in dark corners and basements. No more hiding. They could finally be a real couple.

Her breath caught in her throat when she finally spotted him, strolling around the corner of the cafeteria building. She smiled as she took in everything about him: his tousled hair, his crooked smile. He paused near the door, leaning back against the wall, as cool and detached as ever. Ariana started to raise her hand in a wave.

Then that new girl, Reed Brennan, emerged from the cafeteria.

Thomas pushed himself away from the gray stone wall and fell into step with Reed and her little redheaded friend. He slipped his hand into his pocket and pulled it out again, holding something up for Reed to see. Ariana leaned forward, squinting in the sunlight. The realization of what Thomas was holding settled over her slowly. She watched as Thomas pinched the small piece of metal between his thumb and forefinger.

It was a subway token. Just like the one he'd given her.

Prickly heat raced over Ariana's skin and stung her eyes. She pulled out her delicate gold chain, where the token had once hung next to her fleur-de-lis, and twisted it tightly around her finger. All summer she had felt the absence of that token, the symbol of her and Thomas. All summer she'd looked forward to the day he would return it to her and she could feel the cool weight of it against her skin again, reminding her of Thomas's devotion every second of every day. Now she watched as Thomas rolled the token carelessly between his fingers, grinning devilishly at Reed while he held it in front of her. Just out of her reach.

This wasn't happening. It was not happening. Thomas loved *her*. She knew he did.

But there was no denying what she was seeing. Hot rage bubbled up inside of her. She watched as a warm pink blush surfaced in Reed's cheeks. Watched Thomas laugh and joke with her. Watched as they stopped at the edge of the quad. As Thomas peered into Reed's eyes. Ariana was close enough to see the way he looked at Reed. A mixture of intrigue and attraction.

Ariana's heart pounded wildly. Her dry throat started to close and she had to force herself to breathe.

In . . . two . . . three . . .

Out . . . two . . . three . . .

He couldn't be interested in Reed. This common sophomore. This was some kind of mistake. It had to be.

He loves me. *He's been waiting all summer to be with* me.

But then Thomas handed the subway token to Reed, and the world screeched to a stop around Ariana. He stuffed his hands into his pockets, backing away, still smiling at the new girl. Finally, he turned away from Reed, toward Ariana, the satisfied smile still playing about his lips. Dash and Gage fell into step with him, and they shuffled through the quad, passing just a few feet away from where Ariana was standing.

She had to do something. Had to stop this. The situation was hers to control. She had to be in control.

"Thomas," Ariana called out, her voice strained.

But he didn't see her. Or chose to ignore her. Either way, the pain was unbearable.

Suddenly, Mel's words from that awful encounter in the diner echoed in her mind.

"Everything was perfect. We loved each other. And then one day, he told me that he still loved me, but that things were too complicated between us. And then he found you."

Ariana's gaze snapped back to the new girl, still blushing as she gazed down at the token with her friend as if in awe. This new girl had no idea she held everything that was Ariana's in the palm of her hand. He was leaving Ariana just like he'd left Mel.

A cold, familiar feeling settled over Ariana's shoulders. So achingly familiar it settled her nerves. Reminded her of how naïve she was. How indescribably stupid and trusting and worthless. Even Thomas didn't want her. After everything she'd done to be with him, he'd moved on from her without so much as a word, a glance, a kiss good-bye.

But then, maybe he just needed reminding. Boys were fickle, weren't they? Especially Thomas. Notoriously so. Perhaps, after a long summer away, he just needed to be reminded of what he and Ariana shared. This Reed girl was just a distraction. A plaything. His chance to slum with a scholarship girl. Once he was done with her, he would come back to Ariana. They had shared a special connection. She was sure of it.

But then Ariana would have to wait. Just like she'd waited all spring and summer. And she was sick of waiting.

A few yards away, Reed glanced up and looked right into Ariana's eyes. She smiled uncertainly.

Ariana stared back at her blankly, noticing the way her shirt was slightly frayed at the collar. She wondered if anyone would miss Reed if she just disappeared.